FIC BAK
Baker, E. D.
THE AGNES IRWIN SCHOOL
W9-AGA-845

THE DRAGON *Princess*

Books by E. D. Baker

THE TALES OF THE FROG PRINCESS:

THE FROG PRINCESS

DRAGON'S BREATH

ONCE UPON A CURSE

NO PLACE FOR MAGIC

THE SALAMANDER SPELL

THE DRAGON PRINCESS

WINGS

THE DRAGON Princess

Book Six in
the Tales of the Frog Princess

E. D. BAKER

NEW YORK • BERLIN • LONDON

Published by Bloomsbury U.S.A. Children's Books
175 Fifth Avenue, New York, New York 10010

Library of Congress Cataloging-in-Publication Data
Baker, E. D.
The dragon princess / by E. D. Baker.—1st U.S. ed.
p. cm.—(Tales of the frog princess ; bk. 6)
Summary: Although a princess, Millie cannot keep herself from turning
unexpectedly into a dragon, so she ventures off to the Icy North to find the Blue
Witch, who she hopes will help her learn to control her dragon magic.
ISBN-13: 978-1-59990-194-7 • ISBN-10: 1-59990-194-3
[1. Princesses—Fiction. 2. Dragons—Fiction. 3. Magic—Fiction. 4. Humorous stories.]
I. Title.
PZ8.B173Dp 2008 [Fic]—dc22 2008008016

First U.S. Edition 2008
Typeset by Westchester Book Composition
Printed in the U.S.A. by Quebecor World Fairfield
2 4 6 8 10 9 7 5 3 1

All papers used by Bloomsbury U.S.A. are natural, recyclable products
made from wood grown in well-managed forests. The manufacturing processes
conform to the environmental regulations of the country of origin.

This book is dedicated to Ellie, who likes my crazy ideas and knows when to say no. Don't worry, there aren't any pie fights in this story either. To Kim, who helps me with my Web site and has great ideas of her own. To Pudgy Grumpkins—because. To my fans, for their encouragement and kind words. To Victoria Wells Arms, for believing in me.

Prologue

Though she was just a few minutes old, everyone agreed that the baby was beautiful. She had eyes like those of her mother, Princess Emma, and a shock of blond hair much like that of her grandmother, Queen Chartreuse. Emma swore that her daughter had Eadric's smile, but her mother, her aunt, and her grandmother all claimed that the baby was too young and wouldn't really smile for some time yet.

When she was only three months pregnant, Emma had dreamed that the baby was going to be a girl. After that, she and her husband, Prince Eadric, had never worried about a boy's name. The baby would be named Millie, after the second Green Witch, Emma's long-ago ancestor.

Although Emma wanted to show Millie to Eadric right away, the midwife and all the other women in the room insisted that they wash the baby first. Unfortunately, an overeager lady-in-waiting hadn't bothered to warm the water before bringing it to the midwife. The midwife, rattled in the presence of so much royalty, most of whom were witches, splashed the cold water on the baby. With a startled cry, the baby turned red as a strawberry, and her thin wail broke the calm of her parents' bedchamber. Emma sat up to see what was wrong. At that instant, the air seemed to sizzle and the baby turned from a beautiful human newborn with honey-blond hair into a baby dragon with scales of the palest green. Queen Chartreuse screamed. Two ladies-in-waiting fled the room. The midwife fainted.

Emma sighed and reached for her baby. "I was afraid of this," she murmured, gazing down at the squalling infant. Turning to her aunt Grassina, she added, "This is what comes of spending half my life as a dragon."

One

Not quite fifteen years later

Princess Emma, the Green Witch of Greater Greensward, was sitting at her worktable copying spells onto fresh parchment when a slender green dragon darted through her window and landed on the floor behind her.

"Millie's home!" squawked the green-and-yellow parrot perched on the edge of a precariously balanced stack of books. The bird flapped its wings, making the whole stack sway. Emma gestured at the books as they started to fall, and they shivered back into place.

"I know, You-too," said Emma. "You don't need to tell me when she's standing right here. And as for you, Millie," she said, turning to the dragon, "what upset you this time?"

The dragon sat down and wrapped her long, spiked tail around her. "The scullery maid dropped a pail of muddy water at the top of the stairs just as I was coming up. I'd already put on my new gown for Prince Atworth's visit and the water ruined it. I changed into a dragon before I could help it. Yes, I know you can fix the gown, but I didn't think of that until later. Anyway, the girl started screaming, so I flew out the window. She was terrified—as if she thought I was about to bite off her head. I don't understand. After all these years, why are some people still so afraid of me? I've never hurt anyone while I was a dragon, at least, not since I was a little girl and didn't know any better. You'd think everyone here at the castle would remember that."

"I'm sorry, darling. It's human nature to be afraid of dragons. I'm sure you handled it very well."

Light shimmered around the dragon and a lovely young girl appeared. Her honey-gold hair framed her face in soft curls and cascaded down her back. Except for her dainty nose, her face was much like her mother's and her eyes were the same shade of deep green.

"What a mess!" screeched the parrot.

Millie glanced down at her gown and sighed. The pale green skirt was splattered with mud and the real blossoms sewn onto the bodice were broken and wilted. She touched one of the stems, wishing she could fix it herself. Although Millie had a magic of her own, she was unable to perform the simplest kind of spells that most witches found easy. "Would you mind fixing it for me, Mother?"

"Not at all. I'll just—"

"Zoë's here!" shrieked You-too, and both mother and daughter turned to the window where a little bat had landed on the ledge. "I don't know why we have a door if everyone comes through the window," the parrot grumbled.

"I don't mean to intrude," said the bat. "I was on my way over when I saw Millie come through the window, so I thought I'd look for her here."

"We were just talking," said Emma. "Come right in."

Zoë fluttered into the room and settled on the floor beside Millie. A shadow passed over the bat and a puff of cool, dank air made Millie sneeze. When she looked at her friend again, Zoë was no longer a bat, but a slender girl whose head came up just past Millie's shoulder. Her hair was such a pale blond that it looked almost white; her eyes were blue-gray and shining.

The parrot flapped its wings and squawked, "Watch your necks! Vampire in the room!"

"You have to be the rudest bird I've ever met," said Millie. "I don't know why you keep him, Mother."

"He was a wedding gift from Olefat Wizard to your father and me. I've heard that Me-too, You-too's father, still lives with Olefat and gets more obnoxious every year. Sometimes I wonder if that wizard didn't give us the bird for revenge. The old wizard hasn't gotten his hands on any new spells since the day I helped your great-aunt Grassina make him stop stealing witches' memories."

"If You-too gets too obnoxious, just let me know," said Zoë. "I've never bitten a parrot before. What do you suppose their blood tastes like?"

You-too opened his beak to say something but apparently thought better of it and closed it with a snap. When Millie and Zoë began to laugh, he turned around so his back was to them and hunched his head down into his feathers.

"Would you really want to bite a parrot?" Emma asked.

The girl laughed again, her smile lighting up her pale face. "Don't worry, Your Highness. I've never bitten a bird or any creature larger than a grasshopper, much to my father's dismay. He's disappointed that I'm not embracing his family's lifestyle."

Emma frowned. "How can you do that? Don't vampires *have* to drink blood?"

"Full vampires do, but I'm lucky enough to have a choice. I just turn into an ordinary bat whenever the urge to drink blood comes over me, and then I eat insects. It's the same for the boys and little Suzette."

"How are your mother and the new baby?" asked Emma. "I haven't seen Li'l since right after the baby was born."

"They're doing well, thank you," said Zoë. "Mother sends her love." Turning to Millie, she glanced at her friend and frowned. "What happened to your gown?"

"A minor disaster," said Millie. "I was just asking my mother to fix it. Prince Atworth is on his way here. I saw him when I was flying over the forest. He has a small party with him—only a squire and a page. They should arrive fairly soon. I wanted to talk to you about that, too, Mother. Don't you have something else you can try that might help me? Not a potion, but a spell, perhaps? It would be a catastrophe if I turned into a dragon while he's here. He's the fifth prince to come courting, and I can't afford to frighten away another!"

"I can't believe you want me to try magic on you again," said Emma. "You know my magic never works the way it should on you. I think your dragon side changes it somehow. You remember that potion I gave you the last time a prince came to visit . . ."

"Those green swellings were horrible!" said Zoë. "They were the size of my fist and they jiggled when you moved."

Millie grimaced. "I never told you, but they glowed in the dark, too. Even after I drank the second potion to reverse the effects of the first, the swellings didn't go away for days."

"I still don't understand how Prince Leopold made you angry. He seemed nice enough to me," said Zoë.

"I thought so, too, at first, but then he started telling me all the things he would do to 'improve' our castle if we got married, which meant tearing down half of it. He would have made it squat and ugly. And he criticized everything, from the moat to the shape of the castle keep, and acted like he knew more about castles than anyone else. I tried to tell him that I loved the castle just the way it was, but he told me I didn't know what I was talking about. I kept expecting to feel the change come on, so I was thrilled when it didn't. Then those boils or whatever they were started to pop out all over me, and I knew he was going to leave as soon as I saw the look on his face. I don't want another potion, Mother, but maybe a spell . . ."

"I really don't think it's a good idea, sweetheart. Who knows what the side effects might be. And to do it right before a prince is coming to visit—"

"But that's the whole reason I need your help. I'm never going to find the man I'm supposed to spend the rest of my life with if I keep scaring them away!"

"You still have plenty of time, Millie," said Emma. "You're not that old."

"I'm turning fifteen the day after tomorrow!" Millie wailed. "By the time you were fifteen you had already fallen in love with Father. And just last night Grandmother read a letter to me that she'd received from her old friend Queen Isabelle. Her son is marrying a girl that he just met. She was locked in a tower for most of her life and he was the first prince she'd ever seen. The girl is a year younger than me! Grandmother says that there aren't very many good princes around and if I don't hurry, they'll all be taken."

"Chartreuse always was helpful that way," Emma muttered. "I wouldn't worry about it," she said in a louder voice. "When I was young, she told me that no prince would marry me, and tried to make me marry the first one who asked. And then I met your father, who was exactly right for me. I'm sure you'll meet the right man, too, someday."

"But what if Atworth is the right one and I scare him off by turning into a dragon the first time we argue?"

You-too fluttered into the air and landed on Emma's worktable, his long green tail dragging behind him. "Then you'll be an old maid!" he squawked, nearly knocking over a pot of ink.

Emma frowned and snatched the pot out from under the parrot's wing. "Watch yourself, You-too, or I'll send you to the chicken coop."

"What would a parrot do in a chicken coop?" he asked.

"Who says you'd still be a parrot?" Emma replied.

"Thppt!" the parrot said, sticking out his tongue in a rude sort of way.

"Shoo!" said Emma, waving her hand at him. "I can't work while you're sitting on my table."

The parrot snapped at her fingers before darting to the window ledge. As he flew above the table, his tail knocked over the pot of ink, dousing Emma's parchment. Scowling, she gestured at the ink while muttering under her breath. The ink reversed its flow and ran back into the pot, which righted itself with a *thunk*, leaving the parchment as clean as before.

"Please, Mother," said Millie. "I need you to say a spell. I don't want to be an old maid."

"Oh, all right," Emma said, looking resigned. "But don't say that I didn't warn you." Tapping her finger on her chin, she studied her daughter for a moment. "I think we'll try a different approach. The potion I gave you last time was meant to prevent you from turning into a dragon if you got angry. Why don't we see if we can curb your temper instead?"

"If you think it will work," said Millie.

"I can't guarantee anything, but we'll try this."

Quench this girl's temper
And make her mood light.
Don't let her get mad–
At least till tonight.

"What do you mean 'at least till tonight'? What's so important about tonight?" asked Millie.

"You said that those swellings didn't disappear right away when I gave you the second potion. I didn't want to make this spell last too long in case it has side effects you don't like. If it works the way you want it to, I can always try to make it more permanent."

"That sounds reasonable," said Zoë. "I wonder what the side effects will be."

Millie darted an indignant glance in her direction. "I hope there won't be any."

"I think it's so romantic that Prince Atworth is coming for your birthday," said Zoë.

"It would have been more romantic if I'd met him before this. I'd never even heard his name until his messenger brought his letter."

"Someone's coming!" screeched You-too. "Three boys on horseback. Maybe one of them is that prince."

"Let me see," said Millie as she and Zoë raced to the window. The dragon part of her gave Millie excellent eyesight, but she had to wait until the horses trotted from behind some trees before she could see them. "He's very handsome. And he has dragons on his crest. If he likes dragons, maybe he's the one for me."

"Let's go meet him," said Zoë.

Millie turned away from the window. "Are you coming, Mother?" she asked, her cheeks flushed with excitement.

Emma smiled and reached for her daughter's hand. "I wouldn't miss this for anything, but don't you want me to do something about your gown?"

They were on their way down the curving tower stairs when Millie glanced behind her and said to Zoë, "I can't believe all you have to do to change is think about it. I wish it was that easy for me. I can never change when I want to. Do you know how frustrating it is to have so little control over your life?"

"I can imagine," said Zoë. "It must be awful."

Two

As the prince's party approached the steps, Zoë stood on tiptoe to whisper into Millie's ear, "You were right when you said he was handsome. He's even better looking than Leopold."

"Isn't he, though?" Millie said, admiring his long dark hair and chiseled features. She also liked the flag his squire carried, with the golden dragon emblazoned on its center.

"Greetings," said the prince as he dismounted. He handed his reins to his squire while eyeing Millie and Zoë. "Go fetch the princess, and tell her that Prince Atworth has arrived."

Millie giggled and said, "I'm Princess Millie."

Zoë poked her in the side and whispered, "Did you just giggle? You never giggle."

"I know," Millie whispered back, giving her friend a confused look. "I didn't mean to." She glanced at Atworth and saw that he had swept off his cap in a courtly bow and was waiting for her to notice.

"You may rise, fair prince," Millie said as she held out her hand. Atworth took three steps and enfolded her hand in his. She giggled again when he turned it over and kissed her palm.

While the prince began to tell her how excited he was to meet her and how much he had been looking forward to his visit, Millie fought down a rising sense of panic. She thought the maids who flirted with squires looked brainless when they batted their eyelashes and giggled. The last thing she wanted to do was act the same way.

Emma had stopped to send word to Eadric and her parents that the prince had arrived, but she appeared now and nudged her daughter so that Millie's eyes lost their glazed expression. While the prince spoke to her mother, Millie fought the urge to giggle every time he looked her way. When he mentioned that he was hungry, Emma invited him to join them in a midday meal, even though it was still early.

"That sounds delightful," said Atworth, squeezing Millie's hand, which he still held in his.

A giggle erupted from Millie, making everyone, including the prince, look at her in surprise.

Millie wanted to tell her mother about how she couldn't keep from giggling, but when Emma's glance met hers, she realized that her mother already knew. It had to be a side effect of the spell and, in a way, she thought it was worse than the last one. The swellings just made her look awful. Uncontrollable giggling made her look and feel like a fool.

Millie was trying so hard not to giggle that she paid little attention to what Atworth was saying as they walked side by side to the Great Hall. Her grandparents and her father were already there when they arrived, and they greeted Atworth, gesturing for him to sit beside the old king. Limelyn had always doted on his granddaughter, so he studied the prince with great interest.

It was a simple meal of cheese, cold meat from the night before, fresh bread baked that morning, and berries from the castle's garden. "This is delicious," said the prince as he helped himself to another slice of roast pork.

"Cook is saving the best food for the day after tomorrow," said Millie. "Everyone in the kitchen has been cooking all week for the party."

"You're having a party in my honor?" said Atworth. "I'm surprised you have enough food."

Zoë frowned and leaned forward to see past Millie. "Actually, the party is in Millie's honor. Her *birthday* is the day after tomorrow."

"I see," said the prince, but he looked confused. "How can you use the food for a party when you're in such dire straits? I understand that you have a large dragon population in Greater Greensward. Don't they carry off your sheep and cattle and burn your crops to the ground with their foul breath?"

Millie giggled, although she didn't think he was the least bit amusing. "Why no," she said. "Not at—"

"When I heard about your dragon problem, I knew that Greater Greensward was the place for me. I'm quite an accomplished dragon slayer. I have nearly fifty trophies mounted on the walls of the Great Hall at home. I see that you don't have any," the prince said, looking around.

"We don't—," Millie began.

"You must have different dragons in your kingdom than we do back home. I saw a green one on my way here today. I was thinking how well its head would look on my wall, but since your birthday is coming up, I can kill it tomorrow so I can give you the head as a birthday gift."

Millie knew she should be angry at the awful butcher who had unknowingly offered to present her with her own head for her birthday, but all she could do was giggle. The more she thought about it, the more she giggled. When she tried to stop, her face turned red from the effort.

King Limelyn gave his granddaughter a sharp glance and said to the prince, "Did I hear you say that you kill dragons?"

"Yes," said the prince. "It's a real shame that no one in your kingdom is brave enough to slay them. The beasts must have been breeding here for some time for the dragon population to grow as large as it has. I've heard from travelers that there are dragon sightings in Greater Greensward every day. You may breathe easy now that I've come to help you with your infestation. I'm sure we'll be able to work out some sort of arrangement for my services. Say, half the kingdom and Princess Millie's hand in marriage? I'll rid you of all the dragons and, of course, I get to keep the heads, except for the one I'd give to you for your birthday, my dear," he said, turning to Millie. "You are quite lovely, you know, and not too overburdened with brains. I think we'll get on very well."

Millie tried to stifle a giggle and ended up gasping. "I really . . . don't think—"

"It would help if you could tell me where the dragons' lairs are located. I could find them myself, but the whole thing would go much faster if I knew where to look."

This time the urge to giggle was more than Millie could stand. She giggled so hard that she was afraid she might faint for lack of air. "I have . . . to go," she wheezed. Although she welcomed Zoë's offer to help her from the room, Millie was unable to make it farther than the corridor outside the Great Hall, where she let go of Zoë's arm and sank to the floor. "How long . . . until nightfall?" she asked.

Zoë shrugged. "Eight hours or so. It's summer, Millie, so the days are longer. If you're wondering about the spell, there's no saying when it might end. Your mother was right when she said that the spells she casts on you never work the way she intends."

"I wish I . . . could get angry," Millie said, fighting for control. "I'd like to . . . turn into a dragon . . . and fry him to a crisp!"

"And he'd like to chop your head off," Zoë reminded her. "I hope neither of you gets your wish."

Millie giggled and clapped her hand over her mouth. When the urge had passed, she said in a strangled voice, "I swear, I'll never ask my mother to put another spell on me, no matter what. I was foolish to ask her to do it this time."

"You weren't foolish," said Zoë. "Just desperate. But I think we know one thing for sure now. Prince Atworth is not the right one for you."

"You can say that again," said Millie.

When Millie was finally calm enough to return to the Great Hall, the mood in the room was very different than it had been at the start of the meal. Her mother's mouth was set in a grim line and she was looking at the prince as if *she* wanted to take off *his* head. Her grandmother was biting her lip and watching King Limelyn. Both Millie's father and grandfather were glaring at Atworth.

"Ah, there you are, Millie," said the prince. "Your grandfather and I were just about to seal our deal."

"I beg to differ, young man," said the king. "I was just about to tell you to leave my kingdom and never come back. We don't need you to kill any dragons, and even if we did, my granddaughter would not be part of any *deal.* I suggest you go back to whatever minor kingdom it is that you came from and stay there."

Prince Atworth blinked. For once, he didn't seem to know what to say.

Eadric stood and strode the length of the table. "Let me help you out," he said, taking the prince by the arm.

He had dragged the boy from his seat when Atworth planted his feet and said, "You don't have to give me Millie's hand, or even half the kingdom, but would you mind if I stayed to slay a few dragons? You wouldn't have to pay me at all."

Millie was proud of her father when he said, "You don't have our permission to hunt so much as a butterfly in Greater Greensward. If you even look as if you are trying to slay a dragon, I will come after you myself!"

"As will I!" shouted King Limelyn.

Both Chartreuse and Emma clapped as Eadric hustled the prince to the door. He was scarcely out of sight when Emma pushed back her chair. "I'm going to the top of the tower to keep an eye on Atworth. When he's out of sight I'll watch him with my farseeing ball. If he doesn't move quickly enough to suit me, I'll cast a spell to rid us of him for good. You need not worry about him, Millie," she said, stopping by her daughter's seat. "Are you all right? You look awfully pale."

"I'm fine," Millie said, and giggled. "But I'll feel even better when this spell wears off."

"I'm glad I put a limit on it," said Emma. "Let's just hope it ends when it's supposed to."

Three

The spell hadn't ended when Millie went to bed that night, so she was too worried to fall asleep for the longest time. When she finally did, it seemed as if it was only minutes later that daylight was streaming through her window and her parents were standing beside her bed.

She was still groggy when her mother said, "A messenger arrived from Queen Frazzela this morning, and, well . . . I know you had other plans, but we need to go to Upper Montevista today."

"What day is it?" Millie asked, rubbing the sleep from her eyes. "Isn't my birthday party tomorrow?"

Her parents exchanged a wary look she'd seen all too often. "You'll still have your party," her mother told her.

Millie sat up, suddenly wide awake. "Not if we go to Upper Montevista. It will take days since we always have to travel by carriage when we go there. How can we celebrate my birthday while we're traveling? You promised we could have my party here."

"We promised we would be with you for your birthday," said her mother. "We never said we had to have the party in Greater Greensward. Your grandmother has written asking us to celebrate your birthday in Upper Montevista. Frazzela said that she hasn't seen enough of you lately and has a very special present for you. I'm working on a spell that will get us there today."

"But I don't want to go now. My friends can't come to my party if we have it there!"

Her father put his arm around her mother's waist, as if to give Emma support. "We've already sent our reply, Millie," he said. "We're going to Upper Montevista. As your grandmother reminded us, she and your grandfather are getting old. Who knows how long they'll be with us? People on my side of the family don't stick around as ghosts like your mother's family do."

"Why can't your parents come here if they want to see me?" Millie asked her father. "They've never come to visit us."

"My parents don't like to travel," said Eadric. "Besides, your mother and I would have gone there right after your party, anyway. They're having a problem with sea monsters in Chancewold and—"

"I knew it was something like that. I've been looking forward to my birthday party for months and now you have to spoil it just so you can take care of somebody else's problem!"

"The sea monsters aren't someone else's problem, they're ours," said Emma. "If there's an emergency in Upper Montevista or Greater Greensward, it's up to us to take care of it, but we won't attend to the sea monsters until after your party."

"Why can't you ever think about what I want?" said Millie, her face turning red. "Why do your two stupid kingdoms always have to come first?"

"Here we go again," her father said under his breath.

"It's always Greater Greensward this or Upper Montevista that!" Millie knew she was being selfish and unreasonable, but she was so upset that she didn't care. She was angry, too, and getting angrier the more she thought about how unfair they were being. They were her parents. Shouldn't she come first? Suddenly the air seemed thick, the walls too close. She was glad when she felt the change begin. At least now she could get away. Millie paused to take a breath, and in that instant the bone at the base of her spine lengthened into a long tail, her eyes moved farther apart as her skull changed shape, and her skin prickled as scales emerged. A heaviness between her shoulder blades told her that her wings had come out.

"You're never here when I need you and now you're dragging me off with you so you can take care of *another* crisis!" When she finished changing, Millie was about seven feet long, with scales ranging from pale green to deep emerald. She wasn't a very big dragon, but then, nearly fifteen-year-old dragons never were. "I don't think you care about me at all!" she said, her eyes flashing. Throwing back her head, she spread her wings and flew out of her bedchamber, drawing her wings to her sides only long enough to fit through the window.

As she beat her wings, flying high above her family's castle, Millie was so angry that smoke leaked from her nostrils. She didn't notice the flock of starlings that veered away when they saw her, nor the cows that bellowed and ran as her shadow passed overhead. She was thinking about how much she wished her parents would stay home just this once when she noticed a cottage surrounded by a lush garden nestled on the bank of a river.

Even though it was still early in the morning, a knight in armor stood in a clearing just beyond the garden, swinging his sword and lunging at a dummy made of wood and leather. Millie flew lower, and the knight looked up at the sound of her beating wings. She was in the mood to fight, so, instead of flying away, she landed on the ground not ten feet from the knight and puffed a ball of fire in his direction. The knight stepped to the side, trampling a patch of daisies.

"Good," declared the knight, as he waved his sword at Millie. "A worthy opponent! It's been many days since I slew my last dragon."

"You shan't slay me, fair knight," growled Millie, "for I am no ordinary dragon."

"And I am no ordinary knight!" he shouted just before he lunged.

Millie danced away and the knight's sword whistled past her shoulder. "You'll have to do better than that!" she cried. Whirling around, she lashed her tail at the knight, who leaped nimbly over the tip despite his armor.

The knight grabbed a shield that had been leaning against a fence post and raised his sword again. "Then how is this?" he shouted, as he ran straight at the dragon with his sword aimed at her heart.

Taking a deep breath, Millie exhaled a ten-foot-long flame that hit the shield and flared out to the sides. The knight slowed, but didn't stop advancing, so she kept her flame going until she was gasping for air. She was trying to get another flame started when he swung his sword and hit her hard enough to chip one of her scales.

Startled, Millie gasped and narrowed her eyes, but instead of striking her again, the knight began to dance around the clearing, waving his sword in the air and yelling, "I hit her! I finally hit her!"

"We're not finished yet!" shouted Millie, flaming at the knight just as he raised his shield. Once again, the knight came after her with his sword raised, but this time Millie backed away until her tail was in the river and she had to dig her claws into the bank to keep from slipping in.

"I've got you now!" the knight cried. Just as he lunged at her with his sword, Millie stepped to the side and spun around, hitting him with her tail so that he fell, flailing, into the water.

Knowing that the river was shallow there, she waited at the edge, expecting the knight to pop up at any second. As time passed, however, and he didn't emerge, she stepped closer and dipped her head into the murky water to see what had happened to him. She had just started to look around when the knight jumped up with a *whoosh,* wrapped his arms around her neck, and pulled her in after him. Millie gasped, and her mouth filled with water, half of which trickled down her throat. She could feel the fire in her belly go out as the water reached it. A moment later, she and the knight were sitting side by side in the waist-deep water, each laughing at how ridiculous the other looked as steam seeped from her mouth and water dribbled down his face inside his helmet.

"You almost had me," she said when she finally stopped laughing. "You should have pressed your advantage when you chipped my scale. By the way, you owe me for that," she said, glancing down at the marred surface of her dripping shoulder.

"What about me? My armor could rust after getting wet like this," said the knight, reaching up to pull off his helmet. Millie leaned away from him as the young man with straw-colored hair and laughing green eyes shook his head so that water splattered everywhere.

"Not if I know you, Francis," she said, getting to her

feet. "The spell you put on your armor to make it light probably made it rustproof, too. I bet you never even have to polish it."

"Hey," said the young man as he tried to stand on the slippery river bottom. "I use my magic only to help me be a better knight. I can't help it if . . ." With a startled cry, Francis's feet went out from under him and he landed in the water with a splash.

Millie sighed and reached into the water. Clamping her jaws gently around his arm, she pulled her cousin from the river and helped him climb up the slick mud to drier ground. Nudging him up the last few feet with her nose, she said, "If you give me a few minutes till I get a flame going again, I'll dry you off."

"And risk getting cooked like a sausage in a skillet? I don't think so!" Francis said, scrambling to his feet.

"May I suggest you put a spell on your shoes to make them grip slippery surfaces better? What if you really were fighting an unfriendly dragon?"

"Good idea," said Francis. "I'll see what I can do. So, tell me, what made you mad enough to want to bite somebody's head off this time?"

Millie didn't bother asking him how he knew that she'd been angry. Everyone close to her knew that she turned into a dragon when she got really mad. Francis was the only one who had taken advantage of this and had talked her into fighting with him when she was a dragon, just so he could have the practice. Ever since he was a little boy, Francis had wanted to be a knight more than anything. He had practiced day and night for years, much to his parents' dismay; although he had inherited their talent for magic, he hadn't inherited their interest in it. He was already adept with the sword and the lance, but no matter how hard he'd tried, he'd never been even close to beating Millie before.

Millie sighed and settled on the ground beside the bench where Francis always sat. He was taking off his armor when she replied, "My parents have to go to Upper Montevista to take care of another *crisis*. They say we're going today."

"What about your party?" asked her cousin.

"That's what I asked them. Apparently, my grandparents want me to have my party there. They got me a special present and everything."

"I wonder what it is," said Francis. "Maybe it's another gown like last year, although I don't know why anyone would call that special."

Millie shrugged. "Who knows? Anyway, I got mad because it's so unfair that my parents have to drag me to Upper Montevista when everybody was already coming to my party here, but they don't care what I want."

"Parents are like that," said Francis. "Mine want me to practice my magic when they know how much I want to be a knight. I don't have time for silly things like turning coachmen into rabbits."

"Do they actually do that?" asked Millie.

Francis snorted. "Them? I've never seen them turn a person into anything. I think it's because my father spent all that time as an otter."

"I bet you're right," said Millie.

"So, what are you going to do about your party?"

"I'll have to go, of course, but that doesn't mean I'm going to like it."

Four

By the time she had finished talking to Francis, Millie was calm enough to become a human again, but she waited to do it until she had returned home. She was going to fly through her chamber window and change there, but when she saw that a maid was in the room packing gowns into a small trunk, Millie swerved away and went looking for somewhere private. No one was in the sheltered niche behind the stables, so she changed back into her human form in the dust under old cobwebs and was on her way into the castle when she heard the clatter of wheels crossing the drawbridge. Curious, Millie turned back to the courtyard and was surprised to see the elegant carriage belonging to Zoë's family slow to a stop. A moment later, Zoë stepped out of the carriage holding the hands of her two younger brothers.

"Millie, isn't it exciting?" Zoë said as she hurried over to join her friend. The two little boys with pale blond hair ran to keep up. "We're going to Upper Montevista with you. Papa needs to start his annual visit to all the relatives, so when your mother's invitation came, he decided that we should all go. I can't wait to see your grandparents' castle."

"I'm so glad you're coming!" said Millie, giving her friend a hug. "I hated the idea of having my party without you."

Three carriages belonging to her own family rumbled across the stones of the courtyard, which was suddenly bustling with activity as trunks were loaded and the other travelers arrived. Millie was happy that her grandparents King Limelyn and Queen Chartreuse were going, but she was thrilled when Francis and his parents appeared.

"We got your mother's invitation right after you left," Francis told her. "I packed all my stuff in an acorn I bought at the Magic Marketplace. You'd never believe what you can fit in one of those things. Say," he said, squinting into the shadows beneath the wall of the keep, "is that Great-grandfather?"

Millie yelped and ran to greet the ghosts of her great-grandparents, who had come to say good-bye along with some of the other castle ghosts who were her friends. Although they were hard to see in the shadows, they would have been nearly invisible in the bright daylight, which was one of the reasons they rarely ventured out of the dungeon during the day.

"We heard that you were going to Upper Montevista," said her great-grandmother. "We hope you have a wonderful time."

"I'm so sorry you won't be able to come to my party," said Millie. "I really wanted to have it here."

"We can't understand why Frazzela would make you have it at her castle," said a ghost named Sir Jarvis.

"Just be careful on the road," said King Aldrid. "There were bandits on the way to Upper Montevista when I was alive."

"Don't worry, Great-grandfather," Millie said. "My parents chased the bandits away years ago. I'm sure we'll be fine."

A shadow passed overhead. Terrified, the horses harnessed to the carriages began to rear and scream. Men were rushing to control them when a familiar voice called hello. "It's Ralf!" Millie said as a twelve-foot-long blue dragon landed on the cobblestones.

Emma was reciting a spell to calm the horses when two more dragons landed in the courtyard behind the first. Although the red dragon was huge at nearly twenty feet, the blue-black dragon was the biggest of all. Over thirty-five feet long, it had deep-set eyes that could make even the bravest knights quake. Millie wasn't afraid of any of them. Ralf's parents had often looked after her when she was a baby; they were like a second family to her. "Ralf! Flame

Snorter! Grumble Belly!" she cried, flinging her arms around Ralf's neck before running to hug the others. "Are you coming to Upper Montevista, too?"

"Upper Montevista? Why would we go there?" asked Ralf. "We stopped by to see if you wanted to go swimming in the ocean with us before your party."

"Oh, Ralf, I'd love to," Millie exclaimed. "But I can't today. We're going to Upper Montevista for my birthday. We're having my party there this year."

"Really?" said Ralf. "Can we go, too?" he asked, turning to his parents.

His mother shook her head. "Sorry, Ralf, but you know how Millie's other grandmother feels about dragons. She told her archers to shoot us the next time we drop in."

"I'm sorry, Ralf," said Millie. "I was supposed to have my party here, but there's been a change in plans."

"That's okay," he said, but his ears drooped and his ridge went limp. "Maybe I should give you your present now. Here." Reaching under his wing, Ralf pulled out a small leather sack tied shut with a silver cord.

"Thank you, Ralf," she said. "This is so sweet of you." Millie pulled open the drawstring and removed a handful of bright-colored crystals, holding them up so everyone could see. "What are they?"

"We found them in a cave. You eat a couple before you flame and they make your fire come out a different color.

They're really crunchy and kind of sweet," Ralf said, licking his lips.

"Thanks," said Millie. "I'll have to try them next time."

Her parents gave each other worried looks.

"We should go now, Ralf," Flame Snorter said. "Millie's family is going on a trip and we're keeping them from getting started."

"Good-bye, everyone," said Grumble Belly. "Ralf . . ."

"I'm coming," said Ralf, spreading his wings wide.

"Happy birthday, Millie!" the dragons shouted as they took to the air.

"Thank you!" Millie replied, waving with one hand while holding on to the side of a carriage with the other.

As the dragon family took off, the wind their wings created blew the green pennants off the lower towers, knocked over a half-filled water barrel, swept a young page off his feet, and destroyed the carefully arranged hairdos of all the ladies present.

"They *would* have to come now!" said Queen Chartreuse as she straightened her clothes.

"Is everyone ready?" Prince Eadric asked. "Millie, I need to talk to you." He waited while she walked around the toppled water barrel before saying, "Your mother has come up with a marvelous spell that will take all our carriages to Upper Montevista in just a few hours. You'll be traveling with your mother and me. We have something we want to discuss with you."

"But Zoë and Francis—," Millie began.

"—are traveling with their own parents," interrupted her father. "Go get in. We're about to leave."

She had started for the carriage when her mother cried, "Millie, watch out for the horses!"

A groom was walking a fresh pair of horses to her grandparents' carriage. They were only a few yards from Millie when they smelled her. With flaring nostrils and frantic eyes, the horses tossed their heads and backed away from Millie. She hurried to her parents' carriage and climbed in, shutting the door behind her. Horses had never liked Millie. Her mother said it was because she had so much dragon in her. Horses could smell her dragon side even when she hadn't been one for a long time; they refused to go anywhere near her. Unlike most princesses her age, Millie had never learned how to ride.

When everyone else was ready, Emma and Eadric climbed into the carriage with their daughter. Millie loved hearing her mother's spells, so she listened eagerly while Emma recited the one she had made up just for the trip.

> Horse and carriage, you'll now speed
> Through the countryside.
> Take us to Frazzela's home
> With the smoothest ride.

Slow to a more normal pace
When people are around.
Then hurry up until we fly
Over rock and ground.

Get us there before the sun
Sets on this lovely day.
Take the shortest route you can–
Neither stop nor stray.

The carriage lurched as the horses started out, then settled into a pace so fluid that Millie had to look out of the window to see if they were really moving. They were already outside the castle walls by then and when she looked down the ground was hurtling past. Sliding off her seat, Millie leaned out of the window to see the horses. They were running just as they normally would, but the ground itself seemed to be rushing under their hooves.

"I wish we could fly there," Millie told her parents as she returned to her seat. "It would be so much simpler."

Her mother was idly gazing into the farseeing ball that she always wore on a chain around her neck. Glancing at Millie, she let go of the chain and said, "Maybe we'll be able to in a few years, but the people of Upper Montevista still expect to see us travel like royalty. They accept my magic much more than they used to; it's just that they still aren't ready to see us arriving on a flying carpet. Besides, your father and I wanted to talk to you and the wind can be so loud when we fly."

Eadric cleared his throat and said, "You know we love you very much and we think you're wonderful just the way you are . . ."

"What have I done wrong now?" Millie asked.

"Nothing. It's just that we want you to be careful while we're visiting your grandparents. Please try very hard not to lose your temper. We've done our best to keep your grandmother from hearing about . . . you know."

"You mean that I turn into a dragon? I know that's why we've visited them only a few times. I figured that out years ago. But how have you kept them from hearing about it from other people?"

Emma couldn't quite meet her daughter's eyes as she said, "I cast a spell when you were just a baby. If anyone who wasn't a friend or part of the family came near you, he was struck dumb if he tried to tell someone new about the way you change. Unfortunately, there isn't a thing we can do about it if your grandmother actually sees you, which you must try very hard not to let happen. There are certain things we still can't do around Frazzela."

"She likes fairy magic," Eadric reminded Millie. "For some reason, my mother finds fairies fascinating. It's gotten so she can't seem to get enough of them."

"That's true," said Emma, "but she doesn't like it when

I turn into anything. I had to become a dragon the day of our wedding—"

"Because the trolls attacked the castle," said Millie. "I know. I've heard the story."

Emma nodded. "And ever since then, I don't dare turn into anything when your grandmother is around. She became hysterical during one of our visits a few months later, when she saw me turn into a hawk. She threatened to outlaw witches in Upper Montevista."

"Which she could never do," said Eadric. "Not with all the witches my father has helping his soldiers now."

"But she could make it uncomfortable for them again," said Emma.

"And that's why you don't want her to know that I become a dragon, too? It's not like I do it on purpose!" said Millie.

"Which might frighten her even more. Uncontrolled magic would probably terrify her. All we're asking you to do is try hard not to lose your temper, which I know is very difficult at times."

"I'll do the best I can," said Millie.

Five

They made good time going north, having slowed only twice—once when they went through a small village, and again when they passed a group of hunters who would surely have noticed the speeding carriages. Millie was watching the trees in the forest flash past when water splattered the carriage and they stopped with a lurch so sudden that she slid off the seat and landed on the floor at her parents' feet. A loud moan shook the carriage and another deluge struck with a terrific *splat.*

"What happened?" Millie asked as she untangled herself from their legs.

Her father reached for the door, saying, "I'm going to go see."

There was a series of loud booms and the forest floor shook. If Eadric hadn't been holding on to the door, he would have fallen out headfirst.

“I’m going, too,” said her mother, pausing to give Millie a stern look. “You stay here until we get back.”

“But I want to—,” Millie began.

“Not this time, Millie,” her mother said as she peered out the window. “I don’t need to worry about you and whatever is going on out there, too.”

While her mother shut the carriage door behind her, Millie scooted toward the window. “I’m not a little girl anymore,” she muttered. “I don’t know why I have to stay inside.” Millie reached for the latch when she saw Li’l, the bat, fly out of her carriage, and her daughter Zoë climb down as a human. When she saw her grandparents get out of their carriage, and Francis and his parents get out of theirs, Millie couldn’t wait any longer. A deep rumbling sound was making the trees vibrate when she opened the door and slipped out. The sound rose and fell as Millie crept around the back, hoping to see what was happening without being seen herself. The ground was wet and muddy, so she had to pick her way carefully and didn’t see Francis until she bumped into him.

“What are you doing?” he asked.

“Sh!” hissed Millie. “My mother told me to stay in the carriage.”

“It’s giants,” whispered Zoë as she joined them. “There’s a whole crowd. They’re standing around talking to your parents, Millie. Come here and I’ll show you.” Zoë led the way to the edge of a ditch tall enough for a man to stand in without his head showing over the top. It was nearly twenty feet wide, and on the other side rested a stack of logs well over sixty feet long.

Millie leaned over the ditch, trying to see past the closer trees to where two giants had crouched down to talk to her parents. There were four giants all told, not the crowd that Zoë had mentioned, but even four giants was a lot. Millie thought it must be a family, with a mother, a father, and two boys who were almost as big as their parents. The adults were talking to Emma while the boys stood behind them, each with a hand on his mother's shoulder. Huge tears trickled down her cheeks, which, Millie decided, explained the water that had hit the carriage.

Although the rumble of a giant's voice could make the ground shake, the giants who were talking to her parents were courteous enough to whisper, yet even from a distance, Millie could hear most of what they were saying.

"We were felling trees so we could make a boat," whispered the father. "We want to explore the Eastern Sea. Our friends have already gone to start a new life on one of the islands."

"My Penelope . . . ," the mother cried, wiping her eyes.

The father shook his head. "She's just a little girl. She could be anywhere."

"She's only three," the mother whispered. "I was watching her and I turned away for a minute to catch a tree that was about to hit my boys. And then when I looked for my little Penelope, she was gone." The giantess sobbed and dabbed at her eyes with a cloth that could have covered Millie's bed.

Millie couldn't hear what Emma said, but she saw her pick up her farseeing ball and move her lips. An image must have appeared in the ball, because the giants bent closer to peer into it and were smiling and laughing when they stood up.

"I know where that meadow is!" boomed the father, forgetting to whisper. The trees around them whipped back and forth as if caught in a terrible storm. Twigs and leaves rained down on Emma and Eadric, who clutched each other so they wouldn't blow away. Millie could feel the wind from where she stood, and she had to step away from the ditch so she wouldn't fall in. It was even worse when the giants turned and started to run through the forest. "At least they're going the other way," Millie shouted to Francis as the ground bucked and lurched beneath them.

Trees crashed as the giants pushed them aside, and then there was silence, but it lasted for just a moment before the entire forest shook from the giants' laughter.

"Your parents are coming back," Francis said, and Millie hurried to the carriage.

She glanced toward the trench in time to see her mother move the logs with her magic while Li'l watched from a nearby tree stump. Then Li'l was on her way back, stopping long enough to talk to Zoë. They were already in their carriage when Millie's parents returned.

"What happened?" Millie asked as her parents took their seats across from her.

"A family of giants was felling trees," said Emma. "Their little girl wandered off while they were working and they didn't know where she'd gone. I used my far-seeing ball to find the child."

"She was asleep in a meadow," said Eadric. "You should have seen their faces when your mother told them where she was."

"I'm glad you stayed inside where I told you to," said Emma, leaning across the space between the seats to give Millie a hug. "I don't ever want to lose you the way that mother lost her baby."

"Mama, I'm not a baby anymore."

Emma kissed her on the forehead and said, "You'll always be my baby, Millie, even when you're a hundred years old."

The sun had almost set when the carriages slowed for the last time. Millie stuck her head out of the window as they approached the narrow causeway that led to the royal castle of Upper Montevista. She had been there only a few times in her life and then only for very short visits; all she remembered about the castle was that it was cold, dark, and uninviting. When she finally spied it through the carriage window, she remembered another reason she hadn't liked the castle—it was ugly. Unlike the light and airy castle in Greater Greensward, with its slender towers and many windows, this castle's thick, nearly windowless outer walls and four massive towers made it look squat and heavy, like a fat toad sleeping on a rock.

Zoë's brothers were the first ones out of their carriage. Unlike their father, who couldn't come out of the curtained carriage in the daylight, sunlight didn't bother the children. Millie wondered if the three boys had traveled as bats or as vampires, but either way they shot out of the carriage as humans and with so much pent-up energy that it carried them whooping and yelling around the courtyard. Zoë chased them, calling to her brothers to come back, but they ignored her and didn't stop running until a young man with curly brown hair like Eadric's stepped forward and scooped up the two smaller boys in his arms.

"Who is that?" Millie asked her father as he helped her down their carriage steps.

"That's your uncle Bradston," Eadric said, reaching for Emma's hand. "It looks as if everyone has come to welcome us."

Millie knew who Bradston was, of course, although she had been a small child the last time she visited Upper Montevista and he had been a teenager who hadn't paid her much attention. What she remembered most about him came from her favorite bedtime story: the retelling of how her parents had rescued him from his troll kidnappers. Her mother always finished the story with the spell she'd cast to make Bradston stay close to his mother until he nearly drove Queen Frazzela crazy.

Servants were lighting torches in the darkening courtyard when Millie and her parents joined the people waiting by the door. As the sun went down behind a distant mountain, Garrid emerged from his carriage, although there was no sign of either Li'l or baby Suzette. Eadric had already begun the introductions when Francis ran up to join Millie, leaving his parents to follow.

"That was great!" Francis whispered into Millie's ear. "I wish every carriage ride was like that. I'm going to have to learn that spell so I can use it, too."

Millie turned her head to whisper back, "But I thought you wouldn't use your magic unless it helped you as a knight."

Francis opened his mouth to reply, but Millie didn't hear what he had to say because just then someone squeezed her cheeks between two fingers and turned her head to face forward. An older woman with frizzy brown hair streaked with gray was smiling down at her, saying, "This must be our Millie. My, but you've grown since I saw you last. Of course, if your parents brought you around more often, you wouldn't be such a stranger. Look at her, Bodamin. Doesn't she look like Eadric when he was her age?" King Bodamin didn't answer his wife because he was talking about hunting with Millie's other grandfather, King Limelyn. Queen Chartreuse was there beside Frazzela, however, listening to every word.

"Actually, I think I look more like my other grandmother, Queen Chartreuse," Millie replied between lips puckered like a fish's.

"She does have my hair color," murmured Chartreuse.

"Perhaps," said Queen Frazzela, releasing Millie's face.

Millie rubbed her cheeks as her two grandmothers led the way into the castle. Francis had disappeared and she was about to go looking for him when her father said, "Millie, I'm sure you remember your uncle Bradston." Her father had his arm around the shoulders of the young man she'd already seen. A pretty young woman stood on Bradston's other side, and beside her was a boy not much older than Millie.

"It's nice to see you again, Millie," said Bradston. "This is my fiancée, Lady Maybelle, and her brother, Lord Eduardo."

"Hello, Millie," said Maybelle in a surprisingly high-pitched voice. Millie thought her pale blond hair and light blue eyes made her look almost ghostly in the torchlight. "You never told me that she was pretty," Maybelle said to Bradston. Turning to the boy on her other side, she added, "She might be just what you're looking for, Eduardo."

Taking a step forward, Eduardo bowed to Millie and

took her hand in his. "I've heard wonderful things about your kingdom and your mother, the Green Witch," he said. "Do you have magic as well?"

Millie nodded and swallowed hard. Unlike his sister, Eduardo had dark hair and piercing brown eyes, but he was as handsome as Maybelle was pretty. The look he was giving Millie was so intense that she could feel her face grow hot.

"Maybe we should go in now," said Francis, bumping into her arm.

"Uh-huh," said Millie, but her eyes didn't leave those of Eduardo, who still held her hand in his.

"Did you see where my parents went?" asked Zoë. She was holding her youngest brother, Ivan, who had fallen asleep with his head on her shoulder.

Francis tugged on Millie's arm. "Come on. We have to go help Zoë."

"Why do you let your servants talk to you like that?" Eduardo asked Millie.

"What?" said Millie, confused until she saw where he was looking. "They aren't my servants. This is my friend *Princess* Zoë and my cousin *Lord* Francis."

"My mistake," Eduardo said. "Their clothes . . ."

Zoë glanced down at the simple shift she was wearing, then looked up at Eduardo, her eyes flashing. "We've been traveling."

"If you'll excuse us," Francis said through stiff lips, "we have to go."

Eduardo squeezed Millie's hand before releasing it, murmuring, "Until later."

"Uh . . . right, later," Millie told Eduardo over her shoulder as Francis dragged her away.

As they entered the castle, Zoë said, "I don't like that boy."

Francis frowned. "Neither do I."

"I think he's all right," said Millie, glancing over her shoulder one last time.

Six

Millie was exhausted. Once she reached the chamber she was to use, she lay down on the bed to rest her eyes. It was a cozy room, having been made that way by her mother many years before. The tapestry on the wall and the comfortable bed made it seem like home, and before she knew it, Millie was asleep. She missed supper and would have slept until morning, but halfway through the night her door flew open and a flock of bats fluttered in. Millie sat up, rubbing her eyes as one of the bats settled on her bed and turned into Zoë.

"Guess what?" said her friend. "My parents have to go, but they said I can stay here with you!"

Another bat landed on the floor and a moment later Garrid was shutting the door. He had the same blond hair as Zoë, and the same sharply defined features, but unlike his daughter, the prince was tall and extraordinarily handsome, while Zoë could only be considered pretty. "Li'l said that she can manage without Zoë as long as the boys remain bats," said Garrid, "so I spoke to your mother and father and they said it's fine with them. I'm sorry we're going to miss your party, but at least you two will be together."

"Zoë," said Li'l, a small brown bat, "you can fly us to the castle wall, then I want you to go to bed. You and Millie are going to have a busy day tomorrow, so you should get some sleep now."

"But Mama, I slept all the way here!" wailed Zoë.

"I'm sorry, Zoë, but you'll have to live like a human, at least for a little while. Queen Frazzela and King Bodamin don't know anything about you, so just let them think you're human while you're staying with them." Li'l fluttered around Millie, brushing the girl's cheek with her wing. "Happy birthday, Millie!" Li'l said. "Behave yourselves, and don't get into any trouble."

"See you in the morning!" Zoë told her friend before turning back into a bat and flying out the window with her family.

It seemed as though Millie had just fallen asleep again when she woke to the sound of people running in the halls and the tinkling laughter that could only belong to a fairy. She sat up and was about to get out of bed when suddenly her door burst open and a flood of full-sized fairies poured in as a flock of tiny fairies flew in through the window. Laughing and shouting, "Happy birthday!" the fairies crowded around Millie's bed, showering her with kisses so delicate that she could scarcely feel them.

Tiny fairies began to jump on her bed, shedding fairy dust in their excitement. They didn't seem to mind when a larger fairy swept a dozen or so of them aside so she could sit by Millie's feet. "Happy birthday!" she said, giving Millie's toes a pat. It was the Swamp Fairy. She had become a particular friend of Millie's parents around the time Millie was born, claiming that she had a special tie to them because she had known them for so long.

Millie felt a tug on her hair. The tiny fairies were swarming around her head, vying with each other to arrange her locks in a special birthday style. Not to be outdone, the big fairies began rooting through Millie's trunks, pulling out one gown after another, then discarding them, declaring that they were too plain or too ugly. Her shoes were also dismissed as being unsightly, and tossed under the bed.

When the tiny fairies finally let go of her hair and hovered around her to admire their handiwork, Millie reached up to feel what they had done. Somehow, they had turned her hair into a giant knot that she couldn't get her fingers through. Millie winced when her fingers snagged the knot. "Um, thanks for trying, but . . ."

"Now it's my turn," said the Swamp Fairy. With a wave of her hand, the knots came out of Millie's hair with a *whoosh* and flew in a whirl around her head, settling in an intricate arrangement of curls. A mirror flew out of the trunk on the floor, stopping inches away from Millie's face. She had to lean back to see her hair, which wobbled and bounced each time she moved her head. "Uh, very nice, but—"

"Let me!" cried another fairy.

"No, me!" cried another.

Millie gritted her teeth and tried to look like she was enjoying it as the bigger fairies used their magic to rearrange her hair. Curls, loops, ringlets, braids, poufs, and buns all gave way as her hair changed from one style to the next. From what she could see in the mirror, none of the styles were anything she would actually have worn, although a few gave her some ideas.

"Hello!" called an overly cheerful voice, and Queen Frazzela stuck her head into the room. "What's going on in here?" she asked, smiling broadly.

The Swamp Fairy frowned. "We were just leaving," she said. "Happy birthday again, sweet bud," she said to Millie, and gave her another kiss on the cheek. Then, in a sparkle of fairy dust and a tinkling sound like wind chimes, fairies big and small fled the room.

Queen Frazzela scowled at Millie. "They didn't have to leave," she said, and turned to study the mess on the floor. "I hope you brought a maid to clean this up." Still scowling, she stomped from the room and closed the door with a loud *thunk*.

Millie sighed and slid out from under her covers. Although she could do some simple magic of the ordinary kind, most of her magic was related to being a dragon. This meant that while her relatives could clean a room with a quick and easy spell, Millie had to ask a maid to do it or do it herself. It didn't take long to pick up all her gowns, but her shoes were under the bed and she had to crawl on her stomach to reach them. She was still trying to grab the last slipper when the door opened again and Zoë and Francis came in.

"Looks like your party already started," said Francis.

"The fairies came to see me," Millie said, crawling out from under the bed.

"Is that what happened to your hair?" asked Zoë, stifling a giggle.

Millie reached up to touch her hair. "Is it that bad? I haven't found the mirror yet."

"It's not *that* bad," said Zoë, grinning. "It's worse. Here, let me help you." The last fairy to arrange Millie's hair had left it in stiff coils that sprung from her head like tiny snakes. Taking a boar-bristle brush from the trunk, Zoë brushed out her friend's hair and braided it in one long plait. "There, now you can go out in public without frightening everyone."

"Am I the only one who's hungry around here?" Francis asked.

"I'm famished," said Millie, heading toward the door.

"You would be," said Zoë, as she followed her friends. "You slept through dinner last night. Your mother told us not to wake you."

Millie laughed. "Which your whole family did, anyway."

"That was different," said Zoë. "They came to say good-bye."

"Your parents left?" asked Francis.

"Let's go get some breakfast," said Millie. "We'll tell you about it on the way."

Millie and Zoë took turns telling him what had happened. They were still talking when they reached the entrance to the Great Hall and ran into the witches Ratinki and Klorine, two of the more frequent visitors to Emma and Eadric's castle.

Although they always wore ordinary clothes when they visited Greater Greensward, today Ratinki and Klorine were dressed alike in dark green gowns and short, sleeveless, gold-colored tabards embroidered with King Bodamin's double-mountain crest. Their clothes were the same, but Klorine was smiling as if she was happy to see them while Ratinki's wrinkled face looked sour and grumpy.

"Look, it's Millie!" Klorine shouted in her loud and distinctive voice.

"I suppose this means I should say 'happy birthday' or some such drivel," grumbled Ratinki. "No one wishes me well on my birthday, so I don't know why I should say it to anyone else."

"I gave you a new pair of shoes for your birthday not six months ago," Klorine bellowed, looking puzzled.

"Goody. Shoes," grumbled Ratinki.

"But you asked for them. I thought you liked the shoes! You have them on your feet right now."

"You didn't give me what I really wanted. I asked for you to stop shouting, but that hasn't happened yet."

"Why . . . that's . . . ," sputtered Klorine.

"It's good to see you both," said Millie.

"What are those for?" Francis asked, pointing at their golden tabards.

"King Bodamin gave us jobs. We're his Magic Brigade," Klorine said proudly in a quieter voice that was still louder than everyone else's. "We work with the army to make stronger armor and weapons that don't break so easily. The king gave us space in the dungeon to do our work and another room to sleep in. It's small, but not nearly as drafty as my cave."

"And no one's come to burn it down the way they did my hut," said Ratinki. "I wonder if it's still repairing itself. I should go and see one of these days. Maybe I should let the cat out, too."

"How long have you been here?" asked Francis.

"Two years," said Klorine. "I didn't know you had a cat, Ratinki."

"That's because it's none of your business," said the old witch. "The cat's probably run out of food by now," she mumbled to herself.

"Maybe one of the villagers let it out," said Millie.

Ratinki curled her lip in a half snarl. "Maybe one of the villagers stole it. They always were stealing my food."

"Speaking of food," said Francis, "we're on our way to get breakfast. Would you like to join us?"

"No, thanks," said Klorine. "Three bowls of porridge is enough to start my day."

"I have work to do," Ratinki grumbled. "I want to see if I can find a way to make the opposing armies' spears shatter before they reach our men. Maybe when the spears are in the air . . ."

Klorine nodded. "We could do that. Or maybe before the soldiers throw them."

"Sometimes you come up with good ideas, for a ninny-head," Ratinki told her, as the two turned and started for the dungeon.

When Millie and her friends finally entered the Great Hall, housemaids and grooms were sweeping the floor and hanging garlands from the windowsills. The tables had already been rearranged for the party, with room for musicians on the raised dais where the king and queen usually sat. The only people sitting down were Maybelle and her brother, Eduardo, who smiled and stood up when Millie entered the room.

"Won't you join us?" Eduardo said, indicating the bench beside him.

Millie was happy to share a bench with such a handsome young man. She'd decided that all she had to do was steer the conversation away from anything that might make her mad and see how well they got along when she didn't have to worry about side effects or her fear that she could change into a dragon.

"Where are all the fairies?" asked Zoë as she took a seat across from Millie.

"They went off with some woman named Grassina," said Maybelle. "She said they could help her with the flowers for the party."

"Grassina is my mother," said Francis.

"That's nice," Maybelle said, looking bored.

Eduardo turned so that he was facing Millie, even though she was sitting right next to him. Francis scowled but didn't say anything until after the cook's helper had set a bowl of porridge in front of each of them and returned to the kitchen.

"How long are you staying in Upper Montevista, Eduardo?" asked Francis.

Eduardo looked annoyed as he said, "Are you talking to me? . . . What was your name, again? You have a better memory than I do, Maybelle. What is the boy called?"

"Francis," Maybelle said, giggling.

"It's Lord Francis to you, *Ed*," said Francis.

"That's right! Grassina is the younger sister of Greater Greensward's queen, which makes you Millie's first cousin once removed, doesn't it? As the son of the younger daughter, there isn't much chance you'll ever sit on the throne."

Maybelle clapped her hands and squealed. "Five gold pieces says my brother is right!"

Zoë gasped. "You're both very rude!"

Eduardo turned to face her, his lip curled in a sneer. "You're supposed to be a princess, aren't you?"

"My father is Prince Garrid," said Zoë.

"I notice that no one has mentioned your kingdom. Is it because you don't really have one?"

"Why, I . . . you . . . I can't believe . . ." It was obvious that Zoë was flustered. Although her father was a prince, his subjects were scattered across countless geographic kingdoms. Zoë didn't dare mention that he was the prince of vampires.

"I bet we can uncover the truth before the day is over," said Maybelle.

"My sister likes to wager," said Eduardo.

Maybelle sniffed. "No more than you."

"Perhaps," said her brother. "But I gamble only about things that really matter. And you," he continued, turning to Zoë, "should work on your lies. You aren't very convincing."

Millie no longer found the young man charming. "I can't believe you're calling my friend a liar," she said, sliding away from him on the bench. "Because if you are, you're calling me one, too. I told you who she was last night."

"Ah, but that was a joke, wasn't it?" said Eduardo.

"No more than you are a gentleman," Millie replied.

Francis had two spots of red on his cheeks as he said, "You've insulted my cousin and our friend. You, sir, have no honor. Would you care to meet me on the jousting field so I can teach you a lesson?"

Eduardo laughed. "I don't joust with children!"

"You can't be more than a year or two older than I," said Francis. "I could best you at any weapon you choose."

"Don't flatter yourself, boy," said Eduardo. "You may be related to royalty, but you'll never be my equal."

"Why I ought to—," Francis began, just as a witch seated on the handle of a pitchfork zipped into the Hall, shouting, "There's the birthday girl!" Suddenly there were witches everywhere, pushing and shoving as they streamed through the windows and doors.

Millie stood to watch the witches arrive. Although some of them rode brooms, others rode farm implements, chairs, and magic carpets. One witch even rode a cobbler's bench, which trotted to the corner to wait until its rider was ready to leave.

"Oh, my!" said Maybelle as the witches crowded around, laughing and jostling each other as they tried to get close to Millie.

Smiling until she felt as if her face might crack, Millie returned their hugs and greeted each one by name. Francis and Zoë joined Millie in greeting the witches they knew, while Maybelle and Eduardo shrank away from the witches as if afraid of touching one.

It was some time before the friends had said hello to everyone crowding around them, but once they had, three witches who'd been waiting in the back stepped forward. Dyspepsia and her sister, Oculura, lived in the Enchanted Forest near Zoë's family. Millie had never seen the third witch before. "My sister and I have someone here we'd like you to meet," said Dyspepsia. "This is Mudine. Our cottage used to belong to her."

Zoë gasped and clutched Francis's arm, while Millie's smile vanished. Mudine was the name of the witch who had caught Li'l and kept her tied with string to a rafter in an old, run-down cottage. Li'l had been unable to leave the cottage even after Mudine had gone; it had been Emma who had freed the little bat.

The old witch stepped forward and looked at them with eyes as piercing as a blue jay's. "Where can I find the little witch called Emeralda? She took something of mine."

"I'm her daughter," Millie said, squaring her shoulders and raising her chin. "Maybe I can help you."

"Not unless you can tell me where I can find my bat. I've heard rumors that your mother stole it. Well, I've come back and I want my bat," Mudine said, waving a string in the air. "She was the best bat I've ever owned."

Zoë's already pale skin grew whiter. Her voice was shaking as she said, "You can't have her back. She has a life and a family now."

"She had a life with me," said Mudine.

"She was your prisoner!" cried Zoë. "You can't call that a life!"

Mudine narrowed her eyes and peered at Zoë. "Why do you care so much about a bat?"

"Because she's my mother!" Zoë said, holding her head higher when she heard Maybelle's gasp behind her.

"Well, I'll be!" cackled Mudine. "Don't that just beat all?"

"I'm sorry," Dyspepsia whispered to Millie. "We didn't know she'd act like this."

Oculura frowned and reached up to her face, taking out one eye and sticking another in its place. She glanced from Millie to Zoë to Francis, then sighed and said, "Drat! I was hoping I was seeing all these long faces 'cause I'd put in the wrong eye again. You're supposed to be smiling. We came here for a party, didn't we? Let's get this shindig started!"

Suddenly, the room was a whirl of activity. The air was so rich with magic that it sparkled as witches sent their brooms to sweep the last of the dust from the floor, put up the rest of the garlands with a gesture, and carried the food from the kitchen on a mouthwatering breeze. And then the fairies were there, strewing flowers on the tables and floors, passing out nosegays, and filling the air with laughter. Grassina had followed the fairies into the room and soon the rest of Millie's relatives appeared in the doorway.

Watching Maybelle and Eduardo run off to join Bradston, Zoë said, "I need some fresh air. If I don't go out now I'm going to bite one of those idiots and that would only make matters worse."

"I'll go with her to make sure she's all right," said Francis. "You stay with your guests, Millie. It's your party and you should be here."

Millie was still watching Zoë and Francis work their way through the crowd when Grassina approached her. "I'm sorry your party won't be quite the way you'd planned, but I hope you enjoy it. This is your special day, after all."

"Thank you, Aunt Grassina. I just—"

"Grassina! You haven't changed at all since the last time I saw you," said Mudine, jostling Millie aside. "Except you do have a few gray hairs, and some wrinkles next to your eyes, and—"

"Have we met?" Grassina asked the old witch.

"It's me, Mudine! Don't tell me your memory is going, too."

"Mudine! It's been a long time."

"Sure has. So, I heard that you're no longer the Green Witch. Did you lose your magic, or what?"

Grassina sighed. "It's a long story, but no, I still have my magic." She glanced at Millie, saying, "Mudine and I knew each other years ago. She was one of the smartest witches I'd ever met and knew more about magic than any other ten witches put together. I'm curious though,

Mudine. We thought you were dead. What happened to you?"

"Dead? Ha!" said the old witch. "Though I *was* at death's door for years. I spent my money on one healer after another, but they were all a bunch of fakes. Then I heard about the witch doctor Ting-Tang. I went to see him and he cured me. See, good as new," she said, thumping her chest with her fist. "He was a smart one, all right. Not like the addlepated fools I saw before him. I'd recommend old Ting-Tang to anyone. He can cure just about any affliction. Say, is that girl really Li'l Stinker's daughter?"

"She met Zoë," Millie told her aunt.

Grassina nodded. "Li'l married a prince. They have three boys and two girls. Zoë is the eldest."

"What a shame," said Mudine. "Li'l was the best bat I ever knew. I was counting on her to live with me again. That husband of hers must be something special. What is he, a shape-shifter or a vampire?"

"Actually—," Grassina began.

"Time for presents!" shouted the Swamp Fairy. "Come over here, Millie, and see what we brought you!"

Millie smiled apologetically at Mudine and Grassina before crossing the Hall to the raised platform where the musicians were to perform. The fairies had taken it over, covering the floor with rose petals and decorating a chair with rosebuds. As she passed her family, Millie heard her grandmother Queen Frazzela muttering under her breath,

"Nothing is ready yet. The party wasn't supposed to start for hours."

"You have to expect this kind of thing when you invite witches and fairies, Mother," said Eadric.

Millie caught the angry look her father was giving his mother, which made her wonder just what was going on. And then Millie was at the platform and the fairies were showing her their gifts. They gave her gowns—a few made of fabric, but most made of materials like spiders' silk or moth wings. She received a cape made of violet petals and one made of mouse fur. Three flower fairies gave her two pairs of glass slippers for summer and one pair of heavy glass boots for winter. The Pumpkin Fairy gave her a bag of seeds, each one guaranteed to grow into a full-sized carriage good for one evening's ride. It was the Swamp Fairy who gave her the mice in the wicker cage and the directions for how to turn them into coachmen.

Then it was the witches' turn. Oculura and Dyspepsia gave her a crow that could speak seventeen languages and say the alphabet backward in each. Klorine gave her a magic mirror that would reveal whether a young man she liked was actually her true love. Ratinki gave her a covered basket filled with miniature witches' lights in all the colors of the rainbow. Other witches gave her ingredients to use in potions: fly feet, chicken ears, the eyes of blind cave fish, and the sweat of a left-handed man collected on the second Tuesday of a month starting with the letter *J*.

When her family approached carrying their gifts, Millie already had so many presents that she didn't know what to do with them all. Queen Chartreuse and King Limelyn gave her a new crown decorated with emeralds. Grassina and Haywood brought her books on plants and magic. Millie sighed when her parents gave her a collection of potions, lotions, and perfumes meant to soothe, calm, and relieve tension or bad moods. Of course they *would* give her a practical gift. Then Zoë handed her a necklace of bloodred stones from her family, and Francis gave her a pouch filled with coins from the Magic Marketplace that could be spent only *at* the Magic Marketplace.

"They're worth twice their face value on certain days," whispered Francis.

"What days are those?" asked Millie.

Francis shrugged. "They don't tell you that."

And then Queen Frazzela and King Bodamin were there, saying, "Our special gift for you is in the courtyard. Come along and see what it is."

Millie tried to find her parents in the crowd, thinking they would like to see the present, too, since it was part of the reason they had traveled so far. They were busy listening to a new arrival, however, a witch who was waving her arms as she talked. At Frazzela's urging, Millie left her parents where they were and accompanied her grandmother to the door leading to the courtyard. Until now, she'd forgotten all about her grandparents' promise and wondered what they could possibly give her that would be special, especially since she usually got magical presents and . . . Millie stopped dead at the top of the stairs. The special present was right there in the courtyard with a big pink bow on its neck. It was a small white pony, the very last thing Millie wanted.

"Don't you love it?" asked her grandmother, breathing into her ear.

Millie didn't know what to say. She thought horses were beautiful, but they hated her. If she went near the pony, it would behave like every other horse did when she got too close. It would rear and kick and try to run off and she'd have to pretend not to know why it acted that way.

"It's very nice," Millie said. Crossing her fingers inside the long sleeve of her gown, she added, "but I already have dozens of horses at home." It was a lie. Her parents had horses, but Millie couldn't even go into the stable.

"Really?" her grandmother said, a smile frozen on her face.

Millie couldn't approach the pony without attracting the kind of attention she wanted to avoid. Even so, she felt awful as she turned and walked back into the Great Hall. She just hoped she hadn't hurt her grandmother's feelings.

Francis and Zoë had followed her to the courtyard and they hurried to catch up now. "That was some special gift," said Francis. "I heard your grandparents talking while you were opening your presents from the fairies. They hadn't even decided what to give you. I was there when a page suggested a pony and they sent him to the stable to pick one out."

Millie could feel the heat creeping up her neck. Her grandmother had insisted that Millie come to get a special gift, yet she hadn't even had a gift in mind. Worse, the pony was the most unsuitable gift anyone could have given her. *Calm down,* Millie thought. *Grandmother had no way of knowing.* Remembering her conversation with her parents, Millie took deep breaths until her heart rate returned to normal and her face was no longer hot. "I'm not going to get upset," she told her friends. "I'm sure my grandmother meant well."

The three friends had just walked into the Great Hall when they heard a commotion in the far corner. The witch who had been talking to her parents now had a wider audience as other witches crowded around her. "There were a dozen of them," said the old witch Millie knew was named Burtha. "They were crawling over the river walls and attacking the people in the town. I never heard such screaming in all my born days."

Emma and Eadric looked worried when they found Millie in the crowd. Taking her aside, her mother kissed her on the cheek and said, "I'm sorry, darling, but this is an emergency. Your father and I have to go. The sea monsters are swarming at Chancewold. We've been dealing with them for years, but there have never been this many at one time before."

"But it's my birthday party!" said Millie.

"It can't be helped," said her father. "We have to go. Those people are counting on us."

Millie could feel the pressure building behind her eyes and in her chest, but she was determined not to lose her temper. *It's all right,* she told herself. *They were here for most of the party. At least the rest of my family will be with me.*

"Haywood and I are going, too," said Grassina. "Some of those monsters sound familiar. I feel responsible for this."

"If they are the monsters you created, Aunt Grassina," said Emma, "then it's my fault they're there. I banished them from the moat without thinking about where they would go." She gave her daughter a hug. "Happy birthday, darling. Remember what we talked about in the carriage."

"I'll remember," Millie said through gritted teeth.

No one else seemed to notice when her parents and great-aunt and great-uncle left, because by then everyone was eating. Millie was wandering among her guests, thanking them for their gifts, when she came across Frazzela and Maybelle. She would have continued on if she hadn't heard Maybelle say, "When you told me last week that you could get the fairies to come to a party, I must admit that I didn't think it was possible. Nobody can get more than three fairies at a social event anymore. Here are the coins I owe you. I was sure this was a bet I couldn't lose."

"I told you that the fairies and I are great friends," said Frazzela, taking the coins.

Millie frowned. If this was all about a bet . . . She stepped in front of the two women and turned to face her grandmother. "When did you invite the fairies?"

"Last week," said Frazzela.

"Before you invited us?" said Millie. "How did you know we would be here? I was supposed to have my party at home."

Queen Frazzela shrugged. "I knew your parents would come once I told them that the fairies were expecting you to be here for a birthday party. If you didn't come, the fairies would have been angry and everyone knows you don't want to make fairies mad."

"But you would have made them mad if we hadn't come," said Millie.

Frazzela sniffed. "I knew your parents would never let that happen."

Millie could feel her face growing warm, but this time she couldn't have stopped it if she'd wanted to. "You mean you tricked us into coming? You insisted that we have my party here because you wanted the fairies to come and you knew they always came to my parties?"

Maybelle laughed and said, "Whatever works!"

"Don't act so indignant," Queen Frazzela snapped at Millie. "It's about time you came to see me."

Millie didn't want to lose her temper, but learning that her grandmother had manipulated her family to win a bet made her angrier than she'd been in a long time. Even then, she might have been able to stop the change if she hadn't seen the smug expression on Maybelle's face and the unrepentant look on her grandmother's. This time Millie's whole body grew hot as her heart rate went up and her skin began to prickle. Her eyesight grew sharper, too, until she could see a hair quivering on Queen Frazzela's chin and flakes of powder on Maybelle's nose.

Even in the throes of the change, Millie had enough sense to turn on her heel and start for the door. "Don't you walk away from me again, young lady!" shrilled her grandmother.

And then the change happened between one heartbeat and the next, and a dragon stood where the human girl had been. The last thing Millie heard before she flew through a window was the sound of her grandmother screaming.

Seven

Millie had been flying for hours, unable to decide where to go. She'd considered going to Chancewold to help her parents, but she couldn't bear to face them after having done exactly what they'd asked her not to do. It was almost dark when she started toward home, but she knew she couldn't leave her friends to face the mess she'd left behind, so she turned around again. Finally, when she was calm enough that she knew she could turn back into a human if she wanted to, Millie returned to the castle in Upper Montevista.

The moon lit her way as she circled the castle, trying to find the window to her chamber. Because she couldn't tell which window was hers, she landed in the courtyard when the guards weren't looking. She had scarcely turned into a human when a bat settled on the ground beside her. There was a puff of dank air and Zoë was a human as well.

"I knew you'd come back!" said Zoë.

"I hate to ask, but what happened after I left?"

Zoë sighed. "It was awful. Your grandmother didn't stop screaming for the longest time. She said awful things about you and your mother and your mother's whole family. Oh, one good thing did come out of all this. Maybelle and Eduardo left. I know you don't want to hear what *they* had to say."

"Where's Francis?"

"In bed, I guess. Queen Chartreuse and King Limelyn are planning to leave as soon as you come back. They stuck up for you when Frazzela couldn't say anything nice."

They had been walking toward the door to the castle keep, but Millie stopped now and sat on the lowest step. "I don't know what to do," she said, resting her chin on her knees. "I knew I shouldn't get so angry, but I couldn't help myself. I wish I could learn how to control my temper."

Zoë sat down beside her and put her arm around Millie's shoulders. "And I wish I had some wise advice to give you, but I don't. I've seen what happens when you try to fix this with a potion or a spell."

"I think I can help," said Mudine as she walked out of the shadows.

"We don't want your help," said Zoë. "Millie doesn't need *you* to put a spell on her."

"I wasn't talking about a spell. I know someone who might be able to teach you how to control your temper. She's an old friend of mine. Have you ever heard of the Blue Witch?"

Zoë groaned and said, "What is it with witches and colors?"

Millie shrugged. "They're hereditary titles that the fairies give out. At least, my mother says a fairy gave the title to the first Green Witch."

"Are you interested or not?" asked Mudine. "Because if you aren't, I have better things to do than—"

"I'm interested!" Millie told the old witch before turning to Zoë. "Aunt Grassina told me that Mudine knows more about magic than most witches and that she's really smart. If she has any suggestion that can help me, I'd be a fool *not* to listen. I don't know what else to do, Zoë. I've tried everything I can think of and nothing has worked!"

"I'm not so sure about this . . . ," said Zoë.

Millie looked to Mudine. "Tell me where I can find this Blue Witch. I can't live this way any longer—having to pretend that I'm normal, and frightening people when I don't mean to."

"She lives in the mountains of the Icy North," said Mudine. "She went up there about twenty years ago and as far as I know she's still there. If anyone can teach you how to cool a hot temper, it's the Blue Witch."

"You aren't seriously thinking of going, are you, Millie?" Zoë asked her friend. "For all we know, this might be some sort of trap."

"What do you think I'm going to do to her—tie a string around her toe and hang her from my rafters?"

Mudine slapped her leg and snorted. "That's a good one, what with her turning into a dragon and all!"

"You know about that, too?" asked Millie.

"Everybody in the castle knows about it. Heck, everybody in five kingdoms knows about it now that that chatterbox Maybelle is out spreading the word."

Millie groaned and covered her face with her hands. "What am I going to do? The whole world is going to know that I have a bad temper and turn into a dragon at the drop of a pin. Did you know that my mother fell in love with my father when she was fourteen? If I can't control my temper, I'll never have anyone. I'll spend my whole life not knowing what it's like to fall in love."

"Go see the Blue Witch!" said Mudine. "She should be easy to find. Just cross the Bullrush River and head north past the swamp. You'll come to the foothills after that, and then the mountains. An eagle I know told me that she lives in an ice castle. Shouldn't take you long if you fly, 'specially if you're a dragon."

Millie stood up and straightened her gown. "Then I'd better get started. I want to be back before my parents are, and it takes them only about a week to make sure a sea monster stays subdued, then another few days to let the town thank them."

"Maybe you should wait and talk to your parents about this," Zoë said. "The Icy North is an awfully long way from here. I bet they'd go with you if you asked."

"No, they wouldn't," said Millie. "They'd just give me all sorts of reasons why I couldn't go, and then I never would go and I'd scare away any suitor who came around and end up old and lonely like Mudine."

"Hey!" said the old witch.

"How are you going to get there?" asked Zoë.

"Fly, of course."

Zoë hopped to her feet. "Then you'll have to wait until you're angry again. That should give me enough time to get ready. I have to change my clothes."

"You're not coming!" said Millie.

"Oh, yes, I am!" said Zoë. "You don't think I'd let you go on an adventure like this without me, do you? My mother would never forgive me if anything happened to you because I wasn't there to keep you safe. I am supposed to stay with you, remember?"

"Your parents didn't know I was going on a trip like this. I'm sure if they had known—"

"They wouldn't let you go. Just like Queen Chartreuse and King Limelyn won't once they find out what you have in mind."

"You wouldn't tell them, would you, Zoë?"

"How could I tell them if I was with you?"

"I can't believe you'd stoop to blackmail," grumbled Millie. "Fine, I guess you can come along."

"Maybe we should say something to Francis. He'll never forgive us if we don't tell him what we're doing."

"And how long will that take?"

"Not long," said Zoë. "Any chance you know the way to his room?"

Millie didn't, but a squire flirting with a maid in the Great Hall did. Although the girls expected to find Francis asleep in bed, he was bent over a book on fighting tactics with a witch's light bobbing by his shoulder. When they told him about their plan, Francis put down the book and stood up to stretch. "You can count me in. I have everything I need right here," he said, tapping the acorn he wore on a chain around his neck.

"Why do you need an acorn?" asked Zoë.

"It's like a magical trunk," said Millie. "He got it at the Magic Marketplace. He has all his stuff in it."

"I don't care if it is magical," said Zoë. "How much can you fit inside a . . . Oh, my!"

Francis had unscrewed the cap on the acorn and reached inside with the tip of his thumb and index finger. He pulled out what appeared to be a red thread, but as it emerged from the acorn, the thread became the corner of a red and blue carpet, worn in places but still sturdy enough to carry two people.

Millie was delighted. "You brought your magic carpet! You are so clever, Francis! It's not very big, though, is it?"

"It's perfect," said Zoë. "Now you can go without turning into a dragon first. You two can ride and I can fly."

"But I didn't even say that Francis could come," said Millie.

Zoë grinned at Francis. "Just do like I did and say you'll tell Queen Chartreuse and King Limelyn what she has in mind if she doesn't let you come."

"Zoë!" exclaimed Millie.

"Good idea," said Francis. "But I was going to suggest that she might like to have me along because of my fighting prowess and because I have this." Reaching into his acorn again, Francis pulled out a black dragon scale. "It belonged to my mother, but she gave it to me last year. It can help you find just about anything because dragons are so good at finding things and . . . Oh, yeah. I guess you wouldn't need this."

"Not really," said Millie, smiling in a most dragonlike way. "But you can come with us. Zoë and I would enjoy having your company."

"And my carpet," said Francis.

The royal castle of Upper Montevista was located in the southern end of the mountain range that covered the western half of the kingdom. The mountains were tall, with deep passes between them. A river ran at the bottom of the widest pass, covering a winding trail that had once bordered it.

High above the river, the winds that whipped the

mountainsides were treacherous even at their calmest. Millie hadn't given them much thought before she and her friends started out, but she soon realized that the trip was probably harder at night when they couldn't really see where they were going. While Zoë couldn't fly because of the wind, her bat senses worked just fine, so she clung to the frayed edge of the carpet in front of Francis, telling him when to turn and how far.

The wind continued to buffet them, nearly smashing the carpet against the rocks at times. They tried to fly lower and trace the course of the river, but at the first cry of a hunting griffin, Francis made the carpet rise until it was too high for even griffins to reach. Millie reveled in the excitement of dipping and soaring, of plummeting so that she felt as if she'd left her stomach behind or turning abruptly to avoid an outcropping that suddenly appeared in front of them. She laughed out loud at the thrill of it, the sound of her laughter lost in the roar of the wind.

Although it seemed to take forever to reach the end of the mountain range, it was only just past midnight when they left the mountains behind and entered the foothills. With the winds behind them, Zoë was able to fly on her own and took off from the little carpet. Millie glanced at Francis and it occurred to her from the rigid line of his back and the way he gripped the edge of the carpet that he hadn't enjoyed the ride the way she had.

"Are you all right?" she asked Francis.

"Just dandy," he replied, his voice still a little shaky.

"Thanks for going with me," she said, patting him on the back.

"I couldn't very well let you go without me," said Francis. "You're like my little sister. I couldn't live with myself if anything happened to you."

"Thank you," Millie said, her voice so soft that she wasn't sure Francis had heard it. She understood what he meant, because she felt just as close to him. It occurred to her that she hadn't really been thinking about either her cousin or her friend when she said that they could come. She wasn't worried about her own safety; even though she couldn't turn into a dragon whenever she wanted to, the fact that she was a dragon at times had made her feel almost invincible. And while her cousin had magic, and her friend could be a bat or a vampire at will, Millie didn't feel that either of them was as strong as she was. She glanced at Francis once more, then at the little bat, feeling responsible for them. They may have come to keep her safe, but it would be up to her to protect them.

Now that they were out of the mountains' shadows, the moonlight lit up the night, allowing them to see for miles. Millie was looking at the ribbon of silver that had to be the distant river when Francis said, "What's that?" and pointed at the ground below.

Millie peered into the darkness, trying to see what he was talking about. And then she saw it. A troll was charging across the uneven ground, waving an ax in one hand and a spear in the other. She could hear the faint sound of shouting. "Can you go lower?" she asked Francis, and leaned over the edge to watch the troll as the carpet descended.

At first she had to strain to make out what the troll said, but the lower the carpet went, the better she could hear it. The troll had three heads, one of which was shouting, "I'll flay him alive!" The other two heads roared in agreement.

"Maybe we should see who they're chasing," said Francis. "It might be some poor, innocent human who needs a brave knight like me to protect him."

"I don't know," Millie said. "We can't stop for every little thing. Besides, there's no telling what might be out there. What if it's a harpy or an ogre?"

"We won't know unless we look," said Francis. "As a knight, I'm sworn to protect the innocent. It won't take us too far out of our way. And you don't need to worry. You know I'll keep you safe."

"I'm not afraid," Millie said indignantly. "Oh, all right. Go ahead. See what it is. I just hope we don't regret this."

They found the intended victim stumbling down the far side of the next hill. Rocky outcroppings blocked the moonlight, casting a deep shadow over the fleeing figure.

"I'm taking us lower," said Francis. "I can't tell what he—"

Suddenly, the figure launched itself into the air and

grabbed hold of the carpet, dragging it down to the ground. Millie fell off with an *oof!* while Francis rolled a few yards and hopped to his feet, brandishing his sword.

"Get back, you knave!" Francis shouted. "Or I'll slit your gullet from . . . Oh, it's Simon-Leo," he said, sounding disgusted. Lowering his sword, he reached down to help Millie to her feet.

Millie stood up, rubbing her shoulder. "That figures. What are you doing here, Simon-Leo? Why is that other troll chasing you?"

The troll head with the neatly combed hair scowled. "It was Leo's fault," he said, jerking his chin at the shaggier head. "But then, it always is."

"Can you give us a ride?" asked Leo. "We need to get out of here before old Gnarlybones-Hothead-Rumpkin gets his enormous butt over that hill." One of the two-headed troll's big, coarse hands gestured behind them while the other began to smooth Simon's hair.

"Why did you drag us down?" Francis asked, as the troll bent over to straighten the carpet.

"Simon said you wouldn't stop if I didn't," said Leo. "Hurry up. We've got to go."

"He was right," Francis grumbled under his breath so only Millie could hear him. "Simon-Leo is the last person I would have helped."

"I know," Millie whispered back. "He's always so

awful. Listen, we'll just give him a ride somewhere and drop him off. Then we can be on our way again."

"Are you coming?" asked Simon. "Or should we go without you?" The troll plunked himself in the middle of the carpet, leaving little room for anyone else. Everything about Simon-Leo was wide, from his shoulders to his belly to his feet. He was taller than most trolls, too, a trait he'd probably gotten from his human father.

Grumbling, Francis took a seat in front while Millie tried to find a place big enough to hold her. "I think my mother told me that Gnarlybones-Hothead-Rumpkin is the commander of your mother's army. So why is he chasing you?" she asked, squeezing between Francis and the troll as Francis shot Simon-Leo a dirty look.

"Tell them what you did to him," Simon said to his other head.

"He's making a big fuss over nothing," said Leo.

"The carpet won't go up," said Francis. "You weigh too much," he told the troll.

Simon curled his lip in a sneer. "It's your cheap carpet."

"Or your lousy magic," said Leo. "Try again."

Francis waved his hand over the front fringe of the carpet, muttering to himself. He kept at it until perspiration beaded his forehead. The fringe fluttered, then rose into the air, pulling the rest of the carpet with it. Francis gestured again and the carpet lurched upward, then, with a terrible ripping sound, tore down the middle, dumping everyone on the ground.

"Ow!" Simon squealed.

"My carpet!" Francis exclaimed in an anguished voice.

Zoë zipped down and fluttered around her friends. "Millie, the other troll is coming. He says he's going to rip off their heads," she said, circling Simon-Leo, "and stuff them in—"

"We know," snapped Simon. "He's been saying that ever since Leo played a trick on him. Who's the bat?"

Millie was the first one on her feet. "That's Zoë. We can talk later. We're going to have to outrun the commander."

"He's not after us," said Francis. "I don't see why we have to run." He bent down to pick up the pieces of his carpet, and then dropped them when he saw how they lay limp in his hands. "It's no good anymore. The magic is gone." He glared at Simon-Leo. "You have to buy me a new magic carpet."

Simon snorted. "Like that's ever going to happen."

The three-headed troll was closer now, its heads shouting threats that were becoming all too clear. "When I get my hands on that half-baked . . . ," said one voice.

"I'm going to beat him to a pulp and spread him on my toast!" said another.

"You hate toast," shouted a third.

"You'd better run," Simon told Millie. He was still

talking when Leo, who was controlling the legs, lumbered away. "That dunderhead general won't like that you tried to help us," Simon called over his shoulder. "He could turn your brains to jelly with one solid thump."

"But we didn't try to help you," Francis called. "We'll tell him that you pulled us out of the sky and—"

"You're talking about a troll, Francis," said Millie. "Do you really think he'll care?"

Millie and Francis exchanged a look, and they took off after Simon-Leo. "We have to . . . do something," panted Millie as they started up another hill. "Trolls can run . . . for days, but . . . we can't!"

"What do you . . . suggest? We could . . . go in a different direction . . . from Simon-Leo," Francis said.

"And then what if . . . the commander follows us . . . instead of Simon-Leo? I meant that . . . we should distract them . . . somehow to get . . . them off our trail. I could . . . call a dragon . . . but it might take . . . a while for it . . . to get here."

Francis shook his head. "Don't bother. I have . . . a spell I . . . can use. My father . . . made me learn it . . . in case I ever . . . got into trouble."

Cresting the hill, they had started down the other side when Francis began to recite his spell.

> A dragon roar . . . is just like thunder
> As it rips . . . apart the sky.

Now make it loud . . . so that they'll wonder
If a dragon . . . is nearby.

There was a feeble cough, then a low rumbling sound. The shouting behind them didn't even pause. "Can't you run any faster?" shouted a voice.

"Not with this toe. It hurts!"

"It's our toe, too, you big baby!"

Millie and Francis had caught up with Simon-Leo and were already passing him when Simon said, "That's it? You're using magic to make sounds? A real wizard would have called up a real dragon!"

The rumbling was getting louder, as if a herd of horses was running across hard-packed ground.

Francis frowned. "Give it . . . a minute," he said before glancing at Millie. "Why isn't he . . . short of breath?"

"Bigger lungs," said Millie. "My mother said . . . that's why their chests . . . are so broad."

"I thought it was . . . to hold up . . . their fat heads," Francis panted.

"What did you say?" said Simon.

The first roar sounded like a dragon with asthma, but the next was much louder. It hit them just as they reached the bottom of the hill, knocking them flat on their backs. Zoë tumbled from the sky and lay there, twitching. Everyone covered their ears as best they could, waiting for the roaring to end. When it did, abruptly and without warning,

Zoë shook herself and took off, flying back the way they'd come. Francis and Millie were helping Simon-Leo to his feet when she returned, shouting, "He's gone!"

"Did she say something?" Francis asked Millie.

"Huh?" she replied.

The noise had been so loud that all they could hear was the ringing in their ears. Zoë couldn't hear them either, so she kept talking. "I saw him running the other way. Did you know that he has a stone toe? It shines in the moonlight. I thought it was pretty, for a troll."

Millie's hearing was just starting to come back. "What's that about a toe?"

Zoë, whose hearing had recovered faster than anyone else's, repeated what she'd already told them.

Francis snorted. "What did you do to the commander, Leo?"

The shoulder on Leo's side shrugged. "It was nothing really. I told him that I'd found a leprechaun's pot of gold and let him think he'd bullied me into telling him where it was. When he went to look for it, I locked the door into the mountain so he couldn't come back in. He dug and dug, but never found the gold."

"Because there wasn't any," said Simon.

"And then the sun came up and he couldn't get inside the tunnel so he hid in the hole he'd dug."

"For an entire day," said Simon. "The only part of him that wouldn't fit was his toe."

"Trolls turn into stone if sunlight touches their skin," Millie explained to Francis.

"I know," he said.

"It was his own fault," said Leo. "He should have dug a bigger hole."

"Wasn't your mother mad when she heard what you did?" asked Millie.

"She's off looking for Father again," said Simon. "She told old Gnarlybones-Hothead-Rumpkin to watch us. Gnarlybones told her he would; he likes it when she goes away. It gives him time to plan his revolution. He's been trying to overthrow her for years."

"Simon-Leo's mother is the troll queen," Millie explained to Zoë.

"I know," said the bat.

"Shouldn't you tell your mother what he's planning?" asked Millie.

"She knows all about it. Tizzy says that it's nice he has a hobby to keep him busy."

"Tizzy is one of his mother's heads," Millie explained to Francis.

"I know!" he snapped.

"So, why are you here?" said Simon. "Isn't this a little far north for you?"

"We're on a quest," said Francis. "Millie wants to learn how to control her temper."

"Why don't you just announce it to the world?" said Millie.

"Can I come, too?" asked Leo. "I can't go home now until Mother comes back and that could be weeks."

"Or months," Simon said, sounding sad. "I don't know why Father keeps running away. We miss him so much when he's gone. He has to know that Mother will always go after him. Last year she took us with her. She called it our family vacation."

"Simon-Leo's father is Prince Jorge," said Millie. "That's why his speech is so much better than most trolls'."

Simon nodded. "Our father used to lock us in an old chest and sit on it if we messed up our words."

"Give me a minute," Millie told him. "I have to talk to my friends." Zoë landed on Francis's shoulder and he and Millie walked to the other side of a nearly dead shrub. "I don't think we should let him go with us," whispered Millie. "You know he'll do something to get us in trouble. He always does."

"We can't trust him," said Francis. "Leo thinks it's funny to play nasty tricks on people, and Simon is just nasty."

"I've never met him before," said Zoë, "but he makes me uncomfortable."

Millie nodded. "Then it's settled. He can't go with us. Just don't be mean when you tell him," she said to Francis.

"Why do I have to tell him?"

"Because I'll probably feel bad if I do it, and then he'll talk me into letting him go," said Millie.

"That's true," said Zoë. "You'd better do it, Francis."

"This isn't fair," he grumbled as they headed back to where Simon-Leo waited.

"Why can't I go?" asked Simon when Francis told him of their decision.

"Because we don't have time to waste and you can't travel in the daylight," said Francis.

"But you're traveling now and it's night," said Simon-Leo. "Are you sure it isn't because you don't like me? Most people don't. That's why no one ever invites me to go anywhere."

Francis looked embarrassed. "Well, that's not . . . I mean, we didn't . . ."

"Never mind," said Simon. "You can go without me. I'll find somewhere to hide. Gnarlybones-Hothead-Rumpkin will come back once he thinks the dragon has gone. He'll want to see if it really ate me or something."

"Are you sure you're going to be all right?" said Millie. "I mean, I don't want to leave you in danger."

"Oh, no, I'll be fine," moaned Simon. "You continue on your quest, leaving me here, alone, to face the commander's wrath."

"Maybe we should—," Millie began.

Francis took hold of Millie's arm. "See you later," he told the troll, and began to hustle his cousin toward the distant river. "Good luck with what's-his-name," he called over his shoulder.

"I feel awful," Millie said, glancing back at the forlorn figure watching them go. "We should have let him come with us. I'm going to go back and tell him—"

"That's exactly what he wants you to do," said Francis. "Just keep walking. Simon-Leo will be fine. He always is. That troll gets into more scrapes than a tumbler's knee and he always comes out laughing."

"I suppose," said Millie.

Eight

Millie and Francis were closer to the river than they'd expected. After climbing one more hill, they spotted the water gleaming in the moonlight only a half mile away. Dawn was hours off as they approached the Bullrush River and began to discuss how they would get across.

"If only we had a boat," said Millie.

Francis looked thoughtful. "I don't know about a boat, but I think I can manage a raft."

With Zoë's help, Millie and Francis searched the riverbank until they found a suitable log, which had probably washed ashore during a recent storm. Francis was holding his hands over the log, preparing to use his magic, when something crashed through the underbrush and Simon-Leo appeared.

"What are you doing here?" asked Francis, sounding annoyed.

"The same thing you are," said Leo. "I'm going to cross the river. What are you doing with that log?"

"We told you that you couldn't come with us."

"Is that supposed to make a difference?" Simon said. "My father always says that, too, but it hasn't stopped me yet. Don't tell me you're not strong enough to lift that puny log! A baby troll could toss that from one side of a cave to the other."

Leo grunted. "Step aside, weakling, and let a real troll carry that for you."

He was bending down to pick it up when Simon said, "You can count me out if you're going to lug that thing around. I don't do manual labor." The head closed its eyes and pretended to go to sleep.

"I could lift it if I really wanted to," Francis muttered, as Leo hefted the log into his arms.

"Where do you want this thing?" Leo asked Francis, turning to face him. Millie had to duck as the log swung around, and when Francis pointed out where he wanted the log to go, she scrambled to get out of the troll's way. With Francis in the lead, Leo carried the log three hundred yards to a small protected beach. The log landed with a crash when he dropped it, scaring a flock of sparrows out of the shrubs nearby. While Francis bent over the log once again, Leo went off to rummage in the underbrush for something to eat and Zoë went in the opposite direction in search of tasty bugs.

Millie was sitting on a large rock well out of Francis's way when he glanced at her and said, "Have you ever tried to make a raft?"

"My magic isn't strong enough for that," she replied.

"Your magic would get better if you'd practice," said Francis.

"I do practice," said Millie. "It doesn't make any difference. My mother says it's because so much of my magic is tied up in my dragon side."

"Maybe when you're able to control when you can change, all your magic will get stronger."

"I hadn't thought of that," said Millie. "I hope it's true. So, what are you going to do with that log?"

"Watch," Francis said. Muttering under his breath, he pointed at the log and twiddled his fingers. A moment later, the log shuddered and split in two, lengthwise. Each half then split into thirds. Before the last pieces touched the ground, Francis had made a vine inch across the dirt and wrap itself around the lengths of wood, tying them together into a raft.

"Very nice," said Millie. "You're good, you know, maybe even better than your father."

"My father is great at what he does. He can't help it if his magic isn't as showy as my mother's."

"What's going on?" asked Leo, stomping along the shoreline with a dripping honeycomb in his hand. When he bit into his treat, he didn't seem to notice the swarm of bees crawling on his head as they tried to stab their stingers through his tough skin. Simon was awake again and was eyeing the other head's trophy. Although the food ended up in the same stomach, the head that ate it was the only one that got to taste it.

"Oh, aren't you clever," Simon said in a sarcastic voice as he studied Francis's handiwork. "You made yourself a little raft."

"It's not so little," said Francis. "It will carry Millie and me just fine."

"Here, you want a taste?" Leo said, offering his sticky fingers to his other head.

"From that filthy hand?" said Simon. "It would be like licking dirt."

"Your loss," said Leo, sticking all of his fingers into his mouth at once.

Simons shuddered and looked away. "The things I have to put up with."

"Say," said Francis, "I've been wondering, why do you have normal names like Simon-Leo when most trolls have names like Stinkybreath?"

"You know our cousin?" asked Leo.

"We were named after our mother's great-grandmother," Simon said. "She had two heads, like us. Our real names are Salmonella and Leotuckus. We prefer the shorter versions."

Francis grinned. "I would, too, if I were you."

"What are you doing now?" Zoë asked, landing on Millie's shoulder.

"We're about to launch the raft," said Francis.

"Say," said Leo, studying the raft as he licked the last of the honey from his fingers, "shouldn't that be in the water?"

"That is where it belongs," said Francis.

"I thought so," said Leo. Simon ducked out of the way as Leo bent down and hoisted the raft over his head. "Last one in the water's a bucket of slime!" Leo shouted as he started to run.

Millie and Francis glanced at each other and smiled. A moment later they were racing down to the shoreline. This time they let Leo win.

"Here!" he said, tossing the raft onto the water. It bobbed on the surface, threatening to drift away, until Francis waded in and grabbed it.

"Climb on," he told Millie.

"This looks like fun," said Zoë, and she flew down to perch on the raft.

Millie had one foot on the planks when Leo ran past her and lunged for the raft, landing on the edge.

The raft upended and sank with Simon-Leo facedown in the water. The backwash hit Millie, knocking her onto the shore and leaving her drenched and shivering. Zoë fell into the water and was floundering until Francis fished her out. "Are you all right?" he asked as the little bat gasped and choked.

"I think so, no thanks to him," she said, glaring at Simon-Leo. Francis turned his head away while the little bat shook her wings, sending droplets flying. "Why don't I meet you on the other side?" she said, and took off into the night sky.

"Thanks for asking about me," said Millie as she wrung out the hem of her tunic.

"I knew you were fine," Francis replied. "It wasn't like *you* were drowning."

"Mumph!" said Simon, as the troll stood up, spluttering.

Relieved of its burden, the raft shot to the surface. Once again, Francis had to wade into the water to get it.

"You are such a nincompoop!" Simon shouted at Leo as he ran his fingers through his hair. "Why do you have to ruin everything? I hate the days when it's your turn to control our legs!"

"Sorry," mumbled Leo.

"You take turns?" asked Francis

"Yes, we do, as if it's any of your business!" snapped Simon. "We each have a hand to use, but have you ever tried to walk when you control one leg and someone else controls the other? It does not work, believe me! We decided when we were young that we would take turns. Today was his turn. Tomorrow will be mine and believe me, things will be very different!"

"I said I was sorry," said Leo.

The shoulder next to Simon shrugged. "Whatever. I suppose we have to walk," he said, and sighed.

"I didn't know there was a bridge from Upper Montevista to the kingdom of Bullrush," said Francis.

"There isn't one. We're going to walk along the riverbed. I don't like doing it because it ruins my clothes, but since brainless boy has already taken care of that, we might as well go in."

"I like walking under the water," said Leo. "The fish are so pretty and so easy to catch!"

Millie looked puzzled. "I thought trolls were afraid of water."

Simon looked scornful. "Most trolls are, but when we were little our father used to throw us in the river and hold us under with a stick. After the sixth or seventh time we stopped being afraid of the water. We learned how to hold our breath for a really long time, too. So," he said, turning to his other head, "do you think you can stay out of trouble this time?"

"I don't know why you're always mad at me," Leo said as the troll waded deeper into the river. "I don't get mad when you do dumb things."

"I never do dumb things," Simon began just before both heads slipped under the surface.

Millie stepped onto the raft, but this time she was able to get to the middle and sit down. "Hold on!" Francis said as he hopped on behind her. It didn't take a lot of magic to steer the raft, so they were both able to look around as they sped across the water.

Millie leaned over the edge and tried to peer into the depths but she couldn't see much. "This water is too brown to see through. Where do you suppose Simon-Leo is?"

"Does it matter?" Francis said, sounding glum. "We're never going to be able to get rid of him."

The raft stopped with a sudden jerk so that they both had to clutch at the sides to keep from falling in. "I have a bad feeling about this," said Millie.

Francis looked worried. "We must have hit a rock or something, but whatever it is, it must be awfully big. This is the deepest part of the river."

Suddenly, two hands reached out of the water and slapped the edge of the raft beside Millie. A moment later, a head appeared as well. The river nymph glared at them with her algae-green eyes while her long green hair floated around her. "You can't possibly think you're going to get away with that!" she said.

"With what?" asked Francis. "We haven't done anything wrong."

"You dumped your smelly garbage in my water, that's what!"

"We did not!" said Millie. "The only thing we put in the water was this raft, and it was made from a log that we took out of this very same river."

"I beg your pardon, but I have it on good authority from three trout and a whole school of minnows that you threw a foul, stinky piece of trash in this river and then started across on your spindly little raft."

"We didn't throw any . . . Oh, wait a minute," said Francis, beginning to smile. "Maybe we did, although we don't usually call him trash. His name is Simon-Leo and he's a troll."

"Francis!" said Millie.

"You put a troll in my river?" cried the nymph.

Millie shook her head. "Actually, he put himself in your river. We were as surprised as you are that he wanted to walk across."

"On the bottom," Francis added.

"No!" wailed the nymph even as she dove back into the river, sending a wave of cold water over Millie.

The raft started to move again, drifting downriver until Francis's magic steered it back the way they wanted to go. "That was fun!" he said as they neared the riverbank.

"Maybe for you," said Millie.

Zoë was waiting for them when they finally stepped ashore. She had turned back into her human form and looked like a pretty, pale, young woman. "You're all wet," she told Millie, whose hair was hanging down around her face in a dripping tangle.

"I noticed," Millie said. She sat down under the branches of a tree and arranged her skirts around her. "Just give me a minute to dry off." Leaning back against the tree trunk, she closed her eyes and thought warm thoughts. Her magic flowed through her, warming her from the inside out. When she opened her eyes again, her clothes were dry and her hair was soft and fluffy. She yawned and glanced up at her friends. "I have to take a nap before I can go any farther."

Francis echoed her yawn with one of his own. "We should all get some rest," he said, sitting down beside Zoë.

The sound of splashing water drew their eyes to the river, where Simon-Leo was emerging from the water with an eel wrapped around Simon's neck and a gnawed fish in Leo's hand. "Ugh!" said Simon as he pulled the eel free and tossed it back into the water. Leo grinned and stuffed the last of the fish into his mouth.

The water seemed to boil and the enraged nymph burst out of the river behind Simon-Leo, shouting, "That was the most disgusting thing I've ever seen. Don't you dare come back! That goes for all of you! What that monster did to my poor fish! I don't know if they'll ever be the same again. I'm coming, babies," she cried, and she sank back under the water's surface.

"Who's that?" Simon asked, staring at Zoë as if he'd never seen her before.

It occurred to Millie that he hadn't, at least not the way she was now. "This is Zoë," she said.

Simon scowled at her. "What are you talking about? Zoë is a bat."

"Sometimes," said Zoë. "Sometimes I'm a vampire. You

have two heads. Why can't I have two shapes?" Turning back to Millie and Francis, she said, "I'm going to take a nap, too. You took so long that I did some exploring. I found a cave off that way." Zoë pointed toward the east where the first hint of daylight was graying the sky. "I don't like sleeping out in the open if I can help it."

Both Simon and Leo looked interested. "Good!" said Simon. "I was wondering if I'd have to cover myself with leaves or dig a pit before the sun came up. How far away is this cave?"

"Not very," said Zoë. "But it's kind of small."

"I'll make it work," said Simon.

"See you tonight!" Zoë told her friends.

"Tonight," murmured Millie, and then she was asleep.

Nine

It was late afternoon when Millie woke to the smell of sizzling fish and campfire smoke. Francis was squatting beside the fire, turning the stick on which he'd skewered a medium-sized trout. She watched him for a minute, thinking about how nice it was that he had come. She could have made the trip by herself, but having friends along made it more of an adventure and less of a chore.

Francis turned his head and caught her looking at him. "You're awake. Good. Breakfast is almost ready. Are you hungry?"

"I'm starving," she said. "I feel like I haven't eaten for days."

"Zoë said the cave was in that direction," said Francis, pointing to the east. "I thought we'd eat, then try to find it. We can get an earlier start that way. I was kind of hoping that if we left early enough, we might be able to lose Simon-Leo. If that cave isn't very far from here, we could get a good head start before the sun sets."

"That isn't very nice," said Millie. "He really does want to go with us, but having a troll along . . ."

"I knew you'd agree," said Francis. "Telling him we didn't want him with us didn't work. Maybe this will. And I've been thinking . . . I know you want to be back at your grandparents' castle before your parents return and, well, so do I. My parents are going to be mad when they hear that we went off without telling anyone, but it won't be so bad if we're already back when they hear about it."

"We'll do our best," said Millie. "If you want, we can eat while we walk."

"Good idea," he said, handing her one of the sticks. "Now, do you want to figure out which way they went or should I get my dragon scale?"

"I'll do it," said Millie. "All I have to do is think about it really hard, and it is easier if I'm looking for a place rather than an object. But don't ask me to find people yet. I'm still not very good at that. And don't talk to me while I'm doing this. I've never seen this cave, so it might be a little tricky."

"You sure have a lot of restrictions," said her cousin.

"Francis!"

"Sorry."

Closing her eyes, Millie turned to the east and thought about a cave. Because she couldn't picture a cave she hadn't seen, she imagined something cool and dark with stone and dirt all around it. She cast her thoughts out and down, because it was sure to be underground. Ah, there was something. Keeping the image of a cave in her mind, Millie opened her eyes and began to walk. "You'd better keep up," she told Francis. "This isn't easy, you know."

"I should have used that scale," Francis muttered.

Although it was sunny when they started out, clouds soon turned the sky dark. Millie lost track of time, but they had been walking for at least half an hour when they reached the edge of a bog.

"Are you sure we're going the right way?" asked Francis. "This doesn't look like the kind of place you'd find a cave."

"This is it," said Millie, sounding more confident than she felt. "Just a little bit farther."

As they entered the bog, the ground grew softer beneath their feet and they had to pay more attention to where they walked. Although some people might have been hesitant to enter a bog when night was approaching, the land reminded Millie of the swamp behind her family's castle and she wasn't the least bit afraid. The sun set while they were walking, and with the clouds blocking the moon and stars, they had little light to see by. Millie let her dragon sense take over and continued on without slowing. She heard Francis murmur something under his breath and knew that he was using a spell to help him see.

Soon Millie saw a light flickering in the distance. It drew closer, but she ignored it, for she had a good idea what it might be. It wasn't long before Francis saw it as well. Touching her arm, he pointed to the light, saying, "It looks like we have company."

"Will-of-the-wisp," said Millie. "Don't pay it any attention and it will go away. All they want to do is lead us astray and abandon us in some perilous situation."

"I know," said Francis. "They've been banished from Greater Greensward for years."

Millie kept following her dragon sense, forging a path through the bog, but the will-of-the-wisp began to zigzag in front of them, trying to attract their attention. Eventually, it came so close that Millie could almost see the shadow figure carrying the light.

"Where's this cave, anyway?" asked Francis. "It's a lot farther than I expected it to be."

"We should be right on top of it," said Millie. "It feels like it's under us now. Look around and see if you can find an opening."

When they finally found the cave, it was more like a hole than the image Millie had carried in her mind. Its sole entrance was at the base of a small swell in the ground and it went down and back from there. The space inside was only about three feet high and four feet deep, not nearly big enough for a troll.

"There must be another cave somewhere around here," said Millie. "No troll as big as Simon-Leo could have fit in this."

"Why don't you try finding Zoë?" said Francis.

"I told you that my dragon sense doesn't work very well when I look for people."

"So?" said Francis. "I don't think this worked all that well, either."

"But I can't just . . . I mean, I might . . . Oh, all right. I'll give it a try." This time, when Millie closed her eyes, she pictured her friend Zoë as a bat. Her dragon sense was a little hazy at first, but after a minute or so she began to feel as if she *might* know where to find her.

"I think she's in that direction," she said.

"You mean where the will-of-the-wisp lights are headed?" asked Francis.

"No . . . Oh, wait . . . Yes, I guess so. I'm sure it's just a coincidence," she said, watching the lights float across the bog. There were more of them now and they all seemed to be heading in the same general direction, which just happened to be the way Millie wanted to go.

They fell in line behind the lights, following them around sinkholes and puddles that looked shallow, but that Millie could sense were treacherously deep. Then another set of lights appeared, angling across the bog to intersect the lights that she and Francis were following. Millie had a feeling of foreboding as the second set approached, as if some real danger was coming to meet them. She had just caught the sound of something large stomping through the muck when suddenly all the lights flared, showing them an angry two-headed troll and a bat only yards away. For a moment Millie could hear the shadow figures laughing, then the lights went out all at the same time and she and her friends were left in the dark.

"It's about time you showed up!" exclaimed Simon. "Those little nits have been leading us all over this quagmire, doing their best to get us lost."

"I told you not to follow them," said Zoë. "It doesn't matter how much you threaten them; will-of-the-wisps are never going to take you where you want to go."

"When I get my hands on them, I'm going to rip their heads off and stuff them down their necks!" growled Leo.

"I don't know if they have necks," said Francis. "Or heads, for that matter."

"Watch it, pipsqueak," said Leo. "I'm not in the mood for jokes."

"What happened, did you wake up on the wrong side of the rock?" Francis asked.

"Uh, gentlemen," said Millie.

"He's just in a bad mood 'cause the cave was kind of small," said Zoë.

"I've seen rat holes bigger than that," said Leo. "I had to spend an entire day rolled up in a ball so the sun couldn't reach any of my valuable body parts and turn them to stone. My back is killing me."

"It's my back, too," said Simon. "But my neck hurts worse than my back."

"I bet my neck hurts worse than yours does," Leo said.

The grass rustled. Millie could sense the presence of the will-of-the-wisps, watching and waiting for something bad to happen. She had heard that they enjoyed witnessing other people's pain and suffering, which is why they liked to lead people astray. They couldn't have known that she and Francis knew Simon-Leo and had been looking for him all along. Because the will-of-the-wisps were probably expecting some sort of fight, it was the last thing she wanted to give them, so it irritated her that her friends wouldn't stop arguing.

The pressure was starting to build up behind her eyes when Millie tried again, "Everybody, this isn't getting us—"

"Simon and Leo have been whining like that all day," said Zoë.

"I'd hold my tongue if I were you, bug breath," said Leo. "You should have told me how far it was to that cave."

"And how small," added Simon.

Leo grumbled, "I have half a mind to . . ."

"You have half a mind, period," said his other head.

"I tried to tell you—," Zoë began.

"Please stop arguing," said Millie. "This isn't—"

"Don't you try to tell us what to do," said Simon, with an edge to his voice. "You soft skins think you're so much better than trolls, but let me tell you—"

The pressure behind her eyes was getting worse, but Millie was trying not to give in to it. "I never said we were better than—"

"You don't have to say it," said Leo. "We've seen the way you look at us. That goes for you, too, baby wizard. You think you're something special, but your magic is no match for my strength!"

Francis muttered and a ball of fire flared to life on his palm. Although it was small, the ball was big enough to light up the bog around them. Simon-Leo was crouched on the other side of a puddle, all four eyes reflecting red in the firelight. Zoë darted back and forth between her friends, too agitated to land.

"Care to test that theory?" asked Francis.

"That's enough!" Millie roared, the transformation already begun. She felt her scaled feet sink into the squishy ground and the cool night breeze ruffle the edges of her wings as she rose up on her hind legs to tower above her friends. The will-of-the-wisps' whispers of fear were so soft that she almost didn't hear them.

Although Leo's eyes never left Francis, Simon glanced at Millie and froze. "Leo," he said, "I think you should look over here."

"Why? Francis is just . . . Whoa!" Leo said. "Did you do that, wizard boy? 'Cause if you did, you're better than I thought. Last time you just made dragon sounds. This looks like a real dragon!"

"I am a real dragon," Millie said, shaking out her wings. "I'm also Millie and I did this to myself. I wouldn't be so quick to disparage soft skins, Simon."

Lights flickered back to life as the will-of-the-wisps edged away from the dragon that Millie had become. She turned and looked out into the dark, seeing all the shadow figures, including the ones that weren't carrying lights. Taking a deep breath, Millie exhaled a long tongue of flame that sent them scurrying across the bog.

"Now," she said, turning back to her friends, "maybe we can get going before someone else tries to use us against one another."

Ten

With Millie guiding them, the four were soon out of the bog and headed in the right direction. She waited until she was sure they were safe, then told the others that she wanted to see what lay ahead, and took off into the night sky. After circling over them once . . . twice . . . she flew over the countryside, exulting in the sense of freedom it gave her.

The land beyond the bog was lightly forested, with enough rolling hills to make it interesting. Here and there a village nestled among the trees, giving proof that humans could scratch out a living even this close to the Icy North. As the rolling land became the foothills of the next mountain range, Millie turned around, intent on rejoining her friends. The sun was already warming the ground when she landed and turned back into a human; her solo flight had given her the peace of mind she needed to return to her human form.

"Where's Simon-Leo?" she asked Francis and Zoë,

who were resting sprawl-legged and weary beside a narrow stream. Zoë was a human again and had dark circles under her eyes.

"I found him a cave to sleep in," Zoë said, yawning.

"Don't *you* want to sleep in a cave?" asked Millie.

Zoë shook her head. "I'm staying with you this time. Simon and Leo snore like giants grinding rocks into sand. I hardly got any sleep yesterday."

"We're going to rest for a while and then get started again. Maybe we can lose the troll this time," Francis murmured as he closed his eyes.

Millie sighed. She would already be talking to the Blue Witch if she'd gone alone as a dragon. Having her friends along was great and she appreciated that they wanted to help her, but it also meant that her trip was taking a lot longer than she'd intended.

The rumbling of her stomach reminded Millie just how long it had been since she'd eaten. She remembered how Francis had caught and cooked fish for their breakfast the day before, and not feeling as tired as her friends, she decided to return the favor. She'd watched boys fishing in the river back home, and she knew that they used long sticks with strings on the end. It seemed easy enough, so she went in search of a stick while her friends rested. After tying a thread from the hem of her skirt onto the stick, she made herself comfortable on the bank of the stream. Millie dipped the string into the water and waited. When a dragonfly darted close to inspect her, she remained perfectly still. She watched a squirrel jump from one tree to another, sending a leaf spiraling down to settle on the surface of the water. Then something small and furtive rustled in the underbrush on the other side of the stream.

"Caught anything yet?" Zoë asked, suddenly appearing at her side. Even though Millie was used to how silently her friend could move, it was still a little unnerving.

"Not yet," Millie said, glancing up.

Zoë sat down beside her. "I've never fished before. Is it fun?"

"Want to try it?" asked Millie, and handed her the stick.

They sat there in companionable silence for a few minutes, waiting for something to happen. Millie was getting bored by the time Francis came to join them, yawning until his jaw made a cracking sound. They still hadn't had a nibble.

"I wanted to catch breakfast, but I don't think there are any fish in this stream," said Millie as Francis sat down between her and Zoë.

"What are you using for bait?" he asked. Taking the stick from Zoë's hand, Francis lifted the string out of the water. "What the . . . You don't even have a hook. How do you think you're going to catch a fish on a string?"

Millie didn't like the way he was looking at her. "You did," she said, and tried to snatch the stick back from him.

Francis held it out of reach and laughed. "I had a hook and bait. You don't know anything about fishing, do you?"

"We were just trying to do something nice," said Zoë.

"That's what I get for traveling with two princesses. Neither of you knows how to do anything practical."

"All right, Lord Smarty, since you know everything, why don't you catch our breakfast?" said Millie.

"You won't have to do that," said a voice from the other side of the stream, and then two boys stepped out of the underbrush. "I'm Seth," said the older boy, who couldn't have been more than ten years old. With his blond hair and high cheekbones, he reminded Millie of Zoë's brother Vlad. If the boy hadn't had such rosy cheeks, she would have wondered if he was a vampire as well. "This here is my brother, Johnny," he said, pointing to the other boy, who appeared to be a few years younger. "Our village isn't far from here. If you come with us, we can get you a good hot meal."

"And why would you want to invite three strangers to your village like that?" said Francis. "For all you know, we could be cutthroats."

"Or witches," said Zoë.

"Or vampires," said Millie.

"Naw," said Seth. "We saw you sleeping. You didn't take turns keeping watch, and any cutthroat worth his salt would have known to do that."

"And witches would have used magic to make their

breakfast," said Johnny. "And vampires would want to drink blood, not eat fish."

"I suppose you're right," Francis said, looking solemn. "But you still haven't explained why you would invite us to a meal."

Seth glanced at his brother, then back at Francis. "We don't get many strangers around here. We like to hear news from the rest of the kingdom."

Johnny nodded. "Do you know any stories about brave knights? Or wizards with real magic?"

"I know a few," said Francis, looking more than a little smug.

"Then you've got to come with us!" said Seth. "Our pa would be mad if we didn't bring you back."

"The whole village will want to hear your stories," added Johnny.

"In that case, we won't want to disappoint them," Francis said, dropping the stick on the ground.

Seth crowed with delight. The two boys crashed through the underbrush, then crossed the stream, hopping from stone to stone.

"I'm not so sure that this is a good idea," Millie whispered to Zoë. "We don't know anything about these people."

"I'm too tired to worry about it," replied Zoë. "They're ordinary boys, Millie. They don't have bushy eyebrows like werewolves or the lingering smell of vampires; I would recognize that right away. I really don't think two witches and a vampire need to be afraid of ordinary people. What could they possibly do to us? You and Francis will have a nice meal and we'll be on our way. I'm sure there's nothing to worry about."

❧

The boys hadn't been exaggerating when they said that their village wasn't far. After only a ten-minute walk, they came across a footpath that soon widened into a narrow lane. They passed an abandoned farmer's hut with weeds growing waist-high in the doorway and no sign of any animals. Although they smelled wood burning, they didn't see any other dwellings until they reached the village itself. The houses were made of sticks, with mud filling the chinks in between, and thatched roofs that needed to be repaired.

As they approached the first of the huts, they passed a man armed with a rusted bell and an old, battered sword. He was peering into the woods, but he looked away long enough to nod at the boys and give Millie and her friends a cursory glance before turning back to the trees.

"What's he looking for?" Francis asked Seth, but the boy had seen someone else and was already waving and shouting.

"Pa!" called Seth. "Come see who we found!"

A group of men gathered in front of one of the huts

turned around. One of the men spoke to the rest, then hobbled toward the children like an old man, using a knobbed stick to help him walk. "Who've you got there, son?" asked the man.

"We found them by the stream, Pa. We offered them a meal."

Their father frowned. "Which stream are you talking about?" he asked. "You went into the forest again, didn't you? How many times have I told you not to go—"

"These two are princesses, Pa! We heard the fella say it!"

"Princesses?" the father said in disbelief. "I'm sure he didn't mean real princesses. You didn't, did you?" he asked, turning to Francis.

"As a matter of fact . . . ," Francis began.

The look in his eyes must have been all the affirmation the boys' father needed. Years seemed to melt away from his face and his voice became more animated as he said, "They're real? Who would have believed it? Boys, go tell your mother to add the last of that goat meat to the pot. We got ourselves two real princesses for guests! We're going to have us a party tonight!"

"If you don't have enough food—," said Millie.

"No, no, we'd be honored to have you stay, Your Highness," the man said, his head nodding like a toy on a string. "It isn't every day such fine young people as yourselves come to our village. My name's Jacob," he said as he escorted them into one of the huts. "And you've met my boys, Seth and John. That's my wife, Bernia, there by the fireplace." A matronly woman smiled and nodded, but it was Jacob who said, "So, what brings you to our part of the kingdom?"

"We're on a quest to the Icy North," said Francis.

"Well, then, a good hot meal is just what you need. You won't be getting many of them up there. Now, you have a seat right here," said Jacob, indicating the only bench in the poorly lit room, "and I'll see about getting you something to eat."

There was barely space on the bench for all three of them to sit, but Millie, Zoë, and Francis squeezed together as villagers piled into the room. Men and women, young and old had come to see the strangers. The young men greeted Francis politely enough, but then turned their attention to Millie and Zoë, smiling at them and trying to talk over the din as more and more people arrived. Millie noticed that she and Zoë were the only girls there more than five or six years old. There were adult women, of course, but no other girls close in age. She thought it was odd and was about to mention it to her friends when an old man with an ancient lute appeared in the doorway. Working his way through the crowd, he took a spot on the hearth and soon lively music joined the noisy conversation.

Millie was flattered by all the attention the young men were paying her and was sorry that it was impossible to hear what they were saying. They seemed nice, however, passing a mug of cider from hand to hand until it reached her, and doing the same with a bowl of stew when it was ready. After that, Millie's mug was rarely empty. Although Zoë didn't eat anything, even she couldn't refuse the full mug they pressed on her.

As everyone around them ate, or at least drank, the evening wore on in a haze of good food and better music. It wasn't until Millie had turned down a third helping of stew that Jacob raised his hand in the air and called for quiet. "Now that you've had a chance to sample our hospitality, we're anxious to know what news you might have to share. What can you tell us about the Kingdom of Bullrush?"

"We haven't seen much of Bullrush," said Francis. "Just the will-of-the-wisps and the river."

"I've heard tell of those will-of-the-wisps," said the old man with the lute. "They take you places no man wants to go and leave you there till your bones rot."

"They can't harm you if you don't follow them," said Millie. "Just stay out of the bog or take a serviceable torch with you if you have to go in."

"You don't say?" said Jacob. "And what about the kingdoms beyond?"

"Sea serpents are attacking Chancewold," said Francis. "There's never before been so many plaguing them at once."

"Ah," said one of the young men, "that would be by the sea, then?"

"It's beside the Yaloo River," said Francis. "Chancewold is in southern Upper Montevista."

"I've been there," said the old man. "I went with my pa when I was just a boy."

"What else can you tell us?" asked Bernia.

Zoë cleared her throat. "The giants are building a boat so they can explore the Eastern Sea and what lies beyond."

"Giants are curious folk, always poking their noses into the strangest things," said the old man.

"And the people of Upper Montevista are more accepting of witches now than they used to be," said Millie. "They have some helping their army."

"Those Upper Montevistans always were smart people," said Jacob. "I remember a few years back when . . ."

As individual conversations started around the room, parents with younger children began to gather their families and take them down the lane to their own huts. One couple with a little girl about five years old stopped in front of Millie and Zoë. "Thank you," said the woman. "You don't know how much it means to us to have you here. I'm just sorry that—"

"Now, Ebba," said her husband, taking her by the arm, "we mustn't bother the princesses with your chatter. It's time we got Maite to bed."

Ebba nodded. “I’m sorry, that’s all I wanted to say.”

“What do you think that was about?” Millie whispered as the woman’s husband hustled her out the door.

“I don’t know,” said Zoë. “Maybe she was sorry because they couldn’t stay longer.”

“I suppose,” Millie said, but the woman had made her uneasy.

Over a dozen people had gone home, leaving more room in the hut. The young men gathered closer now and sat on the floor in front of the bench. “I hear you like to fish,” said one.

“I don’t know if I do or not,” Millie replied. “Today was the first time I’ve ever tried it. I wasn’t sure how to do it, so I’m afraid I made a mess of things.” He was a good-looking young man and talking to him made Millie wonder what it would have been like if she hadn’t been born a princess and had lived in a village like this one.

“I’d be happy to show you how,” he said, his eyes smiling into hers.

“Gib!” said his friend, elbowing him in the side. “She’s a princess, remember!”

The young man blushed and looked away. “My apologies,” he said. “I shouldn’t be making offers I can’t keep.”

“We have to go,” Francis said, getting to his feet. “It’s already dark.”

Millie glanced out the door as she stood up beside him.

The room had been so dark inside that she hadn't noticed that the sun had set or that their hosts had lit candles. "I didn't realize it was so late," she said. "We never should have stayed so long."

"You don't have to go!" said Jacob. "I was planning to offer you a place to spend the night. I know we can't offer you anything like you're accustomed to, but we can give you a warm place to sleep and breakfast in the morning."

"We really must go," said Millie. "We need to reach the Icy North as soon as possible."

"Surely you can stay for one more drink!" said Jacob.

"I don't think we—," Francis began.

"Here you go!" said Bernia, refilling their mugs with her pitcher. "You have to have a drink in your hand so we can wish you well."

Jacob raised his mug, saying, "To a safe journey!" Still watching Millie and her friends, he drank deeply and smacked his lips when he'd finished.

Millie, Zoë, and Francis looked at one another. Francis shrugged, and all three friends drank from their mugs.

"To friendly faces and good food," Francis said, prompting them all to drink again.

"I need to sit down," Millie said after taking another sip. The room had started to sway and her head was feeling a little funny. "Just for a minute or two." Sitting heavily on the bench, she bumped into Zoë, who had sprawled across half the seat. With her eyes closed for just a moment, Millie didn't notice Francis slump to the floor, seemingly boneless.

Eleven

Millie decided that her mouth tasted the way her shoes might after a trip through the stable yard. Her eyelids were so heavy that she wasn't sure she could open them, or even if she wanted to. Her mind was blurry, her thoughts fleeting and hard to hold on to as she tried to remember where she was and why she was there. Wherever it was, it wasn't very comfortable. Her back hurt, her ribs and arms were sore, and her neck was so stiff that it hurt to move it even the tiniest bit.

It was a few minutes before she remembered the party the night before and the nice villagers she'd met. They'd offered her and her friends beds for the night. She couldn't recall if she'd accepted their offer, but she must have fallen asleep at some point.

"Psst, Millie!" It was Zoë's voice, sounding rough and scratchy. "Are you all right?" she asked.

Millie shook her head, wincing at the pain in her neck. She was too muzzy-headed to focus on anything for long and had to fight to open her eyes; when she finally got them open, nothing made any sense. While she'd expected to see a wall if she was in a villager's hut or leaves if she was lying under a tree, all she could see were rocks, dirt, and a pair of filthy feet in scuffed shoes. She were wondering who the shoes might belong to when she realized that they were hers.

"Millie!" Zoë said again, her voice louder. "Wake up! We have to talk."

Millie groaned and raised her head, which she hadn't realized was hanging limp until that very moment. It was so bright out that her eyes began to water. She blinked to clear her vision, but her lids felt grainy and rough, making her eyes water all the more. It wasn't until she tried to rub her eyelids that she realized her wrists were tied and she couldn't move them. A rope had been wrapped around her waist and another around her ankles, securing her to something cold and hard behind her.

"I'm over here," said Zoë. Millie turned her head in her friend's direction. Zoë was tied just like she was and secured to a stone pillar. "I think the villagers did it. They must have put something in that cider. I didn't eat anything and the cider was the only thing I drank."

"But why would they do that?" asked Millie. "They seemed so nice."

"I don't know," said Zoë, "but it can't be for anything good. Do you think you can free yourself? Maybe your magic . . ."

Millie shook her head and winced. The movement had made her dizzy and made her head ache. "I can try, but I doubt it will work. My head feels funny. I don't think I can concentrate enough to do my magic yet."

"Why don't you try while I go see if I can find Francis? I shouldn't be gone long."

"But how are you going to . . . Oh, yeah," Millie said, having forgotten for a moment that Zoë could turn into a bat. Things were getting fuzzier, almost as if she . . . A moment later, Millie's head sagged again.

Millie came around the next time to the sound of crunching gravel and the *swoosh, swoosh* of rubbing scales. Her head was a little clearer this time, her mind not quite so muzzy. Zoë was gone—Millie remembered that she had been there—and no one else could have made the noise, unless . . . What Millie had thought was a rock suddenly swung around and looked in her direction. It was a head, covered in dull red scales and attached to a long, snakelike body that stretched nearly twenty-five feet behind it. Millie thought it might *be* a snake until she saw that it had two legs and wings so tiny that it couldn't possibly fly.

Seeing that Millie was awake, the beast studied her in silence, almost as if expecting her to do something. Nearly a minute went by while they watched each other before the creature said, "Why aren't you screaming? The others always screamed, most of them quite loudly."

"Why would I scream?" asked Millie.

The creature snorted. "Perhaps you don't know enough to be afraid. Don't you know what I am? I'm a dragon and I'm here to eat you. Someone tied you up so you could be my dinner. I'm going to bite you and my venom will make you writhe in pain before it kills you. Are you going to scream now?"

Millie shook her head. She wasn't afraid. After all, she was much more powerful than this creature—when she was a dragon. She was wary, however, because she wasn't a dragon now. As a human, she was as vulnerable to this creature's bite as anyone else. If she could hold it off for just a few minutes, she might be able to *make* herself get angry.

"You're not really a dragon, so I don't know why you call yourself one. I know a good number of dragons. They all have real wings and can fly. I've heard about creatures like you. You're a knucker."

"My, aren't we the expert?" said the knucker. "It doesn't matter what you call me, I can still kill you with one bite."

"I thought knuckers ate rabbits and deer."

"Or stray children. I ate a few, then got a real taste for them. When the villagers kept them at home, I destroyed a few of their hovels and told them they had to give me a girl a week or I'd destroy their village and kill them all. The silly things begged and groveled until I couldn't take it anymore. I'm a kindhearted beast under this scaly exterior, so I made a deal with them. I told them I'd eat their children until they gave me a princess or two. I've heard that princesses are sweet and very tender. But I'm sure that will never happen. There hasn't been a princess around here in years."

The knucker began to scratch at the ground with his talons and it took Millie a moment to realize that he was toying with old bones, all with deep grooves that could only be the marks of knucker teeth. Millie tried to get mad by thinking about the villagers and how they had betrayed her and her friends. But she couldn't get too angry with them. The bones scattered around the pillars showed just how many loved ones the villagers had already lost.

"I tried eating the younger ones, but now I eat only the girls of a certain age," said the knucker. "Too young and they don't have enough meat on their bones. Too old and they're tough and stringy. You look to be just about right," he said, eyeing Millie with appreciation. "Are you ready to scream yet? I'd enjoy eating you more if you screamed. You'd get your juices flowing then. I really like that in my food."

"I'm not afraid of you," said Millie. "I would be if you were a dragon. Of course, if you were a dragon, you could fly away from here and find your own princesses."

"Pha! Flying is overrated."

"You're just saying that because you can't do it. Why, I've seen dragons at the Dragon Olympics who could do the most beautiful loops and spins. And the flames! Why, Flame Snorter can breathe a flame nearly a hundred feet long."

"Aha!" shouted the knucker. "I thought there was something about you! Your smell alone would give you away. You wear their stench like a bad perfume. If you've gone to the Olympics, you must be friends with the big dragons. They're soft-brained fools to befriend humans like you. They couldn't be any dumber if they tried!"

"How can you say such things?" said Millie, not noticing her skin beginning to prickle and the pressure growing behind her eyes. "They are the smartest, most bighearted creatures in all the kingdoms. Compared to them, you're nothing but a newt!"

"A newt!" shrilled the knucker. "How dare you? I get sick to my stomach just thinking about those high-and-mighty dragons giving themselves airs when everybody knows that they crawl out of their shell one leg at a time, just like everybody else. And I've heard talk about your friend Flame Snorter. She eats gunga beans and hot flami-peppers to stoke up her fire. If that isn't cheating, I'd like to know what is!"

"Flame Snorter is not a cheater," Millie growled as the pressure filled her head and made her spine feel like it was burning. "All the dragons at the Olympics eat gunga beans and hot flami-peppers. If you had ever gone, you would know that."

Millie's skull was already changing shape as the knucker cried, "Are you calling me a liar? I've changed my mind. I'm not going to wait for you to scream. One bite and you'll scream, anyway. What are you doing? No, you can't . . . That's not possible!"

The ropes broke with a loud *snap* as Millie's muscles grew. She stretched her neck, arching it over the knucker. Knowing that her wings were impressive, she opened them behind her and fanned the air. "You were wrong," she breathed, letting a trickle of smoke escape from between her teeth. "I'm not a Dragon Friend. I'm *one* of those soft-brained fools. And guess what? I eat gunga beans and hot flami-peppers, too. That must mean I'm a cheater. Want to see how far I can breathe my flame?"

"I never s-said . . . I-I mean, I didn't know . . . H-how could you . . . ?" stuttered the knucker.

Millie narrowed her eyes and bent down so that her nose was almost touching his. "I would run if I were you," she whispered in a menacing voice. "And never come back here again. If I ever hear that you or any of your kind are hurting these people, I will hunt you down. I might even get my friends to help me. Maybe we can make a contest out of it. You'd better go now. I'm giving you to the count of three and not one second longer."

The knucker ran so fast that by the time Millie had counted to three all she could see of him was the dust he'd stirred up. Inhaling deeply, Millie shot her flame down the path he'd taken. The stream of fire turned the bones on the ground to ash, crisped the grass, and licked the ground fifty feet away. Millie thought she heard a pained yelp, but she decided that it was probably just wishful thinking.

Beating her wings, Millie rose into the air. She could see the knucker now, tearing across the countryside as it headed toward the bog in the distance. Millie wondered who would suffer more if the knucker were to meet the will-of-the-wisps. She was still feeling good when she dipped one wing and turned in the direction of the only village she could see. It looked tiny from a distance and not much bigger as she got closer.

Millie was looking for her friends, but she wasn't surprised when a villager spotted her first. The sentry at the end of the lane near where they'd entered the village the day before saw her and began to ring the bell. Dragons have excellent eyesight and Millie could see the look of terror on his face. While she couldn't be angry with the villagers for what they'd done, she didn't have to like them and it gave her a certain sense of satisfaction to have gotten her revenge against them, no matter how small.

She was circling over the village, watching everyone run for cover, when she saw Zoë flying out to meet her. Certain that her friend would follow, Millie flew just far enough from the village that no one could see her and landed on the ground with a sigh.

"Did you use your magic to get free?" asked Zoë, settling on Millie's shoulder.

"I guess you could say that," said Millie. "Have you found Francis? They didn't hurt him, did they?" Although she hadn't been seeking revenge against the villagers, the thought that they might have hurt her cousin made her consider changing her mind.

"He's fine," Zoë said. "They tied him up and left him in a cowshed. He told me that they told him they were going to let him out tonight."

"After they were sure we'd both been eaten," said Millie.

"Probably," said Zoë. "Francis feels just awful that you and I were taken. He was still unconscious when I found him and he felt sick when I told him what the villagers had done. I told him that we were all right, but he feels like such a failure. You know how much he wanted to be our protector. To top it off, he wants to be an invincible knight, but now he's sure that everyone is going to know how easy it was to trick him."

"I have an idea," said Millie. "Francis has his armor in the acorn. Tell him to put it on and go to the center of town. I'll meet him there when he's ready. He'll know what to do after that."

Millie waited until she was sure that Francis had gotten ready before she returned to the village. No one else was outside when she saw him standing in the middle of the lane, brandishing his sword. Cupping her wings, she landed ten yards away and roared, fluttering the thatch on the nearby roofs and knocking over a pitchfork and a scythe left leaning against a wall. Doors that had been open a crack slammed shut. Somewhere a small child whimpered.

Francis's helmet clanked when he nodded at her in salute. Raising his sword, he took two steps and shouted, "Have at it, foul beast. You'll torment these kind people no longer!"

Determined to put on a good show, Millie took a deep breath and exhaled flame at Francis, being careful to keep her fire away from the too-flammable huts. Her cousin danced aside easily. Holding up his shield, he advanced on Millie with his sword aimed at her heart. Millie flamed again. The fire hit the center of the shield, flowed to the edges, and shot off the sides in every direction. Francis kept coming. When he was almost close enough to touch, Millie whirled around, lashing at him with her powerful tail. Francis leaped over her tail and somersaulted out of the way. Someone cheered in one of the houses behind her, stopping abruptly when Millie turned to look.

On his feet again, Francis aimed his sword at Millie's neck. "Come closer that I can separate your head from the rest of your body," he commanded.

"Come and get me, if you can," rumbled Millie. Taking another deep breath, she waited until he was in position, then blew a tongue of flame that she let grow feeble and die.

"The dragon's losing its fire," a villager said from a partially opened door. "The knight might have a chance after all!"

Francis may have heard the man, because he lunged at Millie and continued to chase her when she darted out of the way. "I have you now!" he shouted as they ran through the village and out the other side. Once the forest hid them from sight, they slowed to a walk. Francis called out and slapped the flat of his sword against his armor to make the sounds of battle, while Millie roared and puffed smoke into the air so it could be seen above the trees.

"I'm getting tired," Francis finally said. "Do you mind if we end this now? A little bit of blood would be really convincing."

"Forget it, Francis," said Millie. "There's no way I'm going to let you poke me with your sword. Why don't we try this instead?" With a final roar of anguish and a great puff of smoke, she rose into the air and flew in the direction of the village, letting one leg dangle limply and doing her best to make her flying look ragged and uneven. Hearing the villagers cheer below her, she let her head droop and flew off even more slowly, landing when she saw Zoë.

Her friend was a human once again when Millie found her. "Francis said he'd meet us here," Zoë said.

"I hope he appreciates this," grumbled Millie as she sat down with a sigh. "This is the last time I'm going out of my way to make anyone look like a hero."

Twelve

They made good time by walking most of the day and well into the night and didn't stop until they had reached the foothills at the base of the snow-cloaked mountains. Francis was delighted that they had lost Simon-Leo, although Millie kept expecting the troll to reappear.

Even from a distance the mountains exuded a bone-chilling cold that only got worse as the night wore on. Although they didn't want to attract attention, they decided to build a fire to chase away the cold.

"You should have seen their faces when they came out of their huts," said Francis as he tossed another log onto the fire. "I've never seen happier or more surprised people."

Seated on the other side of the fire, Millie nodded. "And you didn't even need my blood to prove to them that you were a hero."

"I didn't want your blood," Francis said. "*Any* blood would have done just fine."

"He wanted to stab me with his sword just so he'd be more convincing," Millie said, turning to Zoë.

"I did not!"

"You were telling us about the villagers?" prompted Zoë. She shivered and pulled her cloak closer around her. She didn't like the cold and this was more intense than anything they'd felt before.

Francis pulled a blanket out of his acorn and draped it around her shoulders and then sat beside Zoë and took her hands in his to warm them. "They cheered for me," he said. "I'm surprised you didn't hear them. Some of them slapped me on my back until they hurt their hands on my armor. They wanted me to stay to celebrate, but I told them I couldn't."

"We know what happens when you celebrate with them," muttered Millie.

Francis shook his head. "They promised me that they aren't going to do that anymore. They won't need to since they think I killed the dragon."

"And I chased off the real human-killer," said Millie. "It wasn't a dragon, it was a knucker."

"The villagers believed it was a dragon and that's what counts. Say, I thought knuckers ate things like vermin and farm animals," said Francis.

Millie shrugged. "This one had acquired a taste for humans, too."

"The villagers made me promise that I'd go back and visit them someday," Francis added.

"That's fine," Millie said, "as long as you understand that Zoë and I will not be going with you. As far as the villagers know, that knucker ate us, bones and all."

"They said they felt bad about that, especially since they thought I'd killed the beast."

"Shh!" said Zoë. "Did you hear something?"

"Just my stomach growling," Francis said.

"No, it was over there in those trees."

"I don't see anything," said Millie.

"I don't, either," Zoë said, "but I could have sworn . . ."

"What's that?" Millie squeaked.

An enormous shape had appeared seemingly out of nowhere, breathing heavily and waving its arms over its huge head. Francis dropped Zoë's hands and reached for his sword.

"There you are!" rumbled a voice.

Millie was the first to realize who it was. "Simon-Leo! You found us," she said.

"Not again!" muttered Francis.

"My mother taught us how to track people," Leo said. "Sometimes she'd let our father go just so we could practice. You didn't think I was gone for good, did you?"

Millie sighed. "Of course not," she said, darting a glance at Francis, who was mumbling to himself. "But we've had a very eventful time since we saw you last. We were tricked . . ."

Zoë nodded. "And drugged . . ."

"And tied up," said Francis.

"Good," said Simon. "I was hoping it was something like that."

"You said they'd run off and left us on purpose!" said Leo. The hand closest to him reached up and wiped a tear from his eye. "You said they didn't want us around, just like everybody else."

One shoulder shrugged. "I wasn't sure," Simon said.

"Then you shouldn't have said it!" said Leo.

"Sit down and tell us how you found us," Millie said before the heads could really start to fight.

"We followed your footprints for a time," said Simon as the troll plopped down on the ground between Millie and Zoë.

"You mean I followed their footprints!" Leo exclaimed. "You fell asleep again."

"It was boring," said Simon. "So, what do you have to eat? I haven't eaten in days. Leo devoured every toad we found last night and our stomach has been sour ever since."

Francis didn't want to share his food with the troll, but he looked into his acorn when Millie insisted. He was still rooting around when Millie felt a prickling on the back of her neck. She looked up and saw that Zoë was peering over her shoulder, and looking just as uneasy as she felt. "Do you feel it, too?" Millie whispered.

Zoë nodded. "Someone is watching us. I noticed it before, but then when Simon-Leo came I thought it had been him."

"Here's an apple," said Francis as he handed the fruit to Simon.

"Is it poisonous?" asked Leo. "They give us indigestion. Our father used to give them to us before we went to bed at night. He said our stomachaches were all in our heads."

"As far as I know, the apples are fine," said Francis.

"It might be the villagers," Zoë whispered. "Maybe they followed Francis."

"Maybe," said Millie.

"I'm going to take a nap," said Leo. "Simon, it's your turn to stay awake."

"Thanks a lot," Simon grumbled. A few minutes passed before he spoke again. Glancing from one huddled figure to the next he said, "Why are we sitting here wasting the dark when we could be walking?"

The only response was the crackling of the wood in the fire.

❧

When Millie woke, snow was hissing softly as it fell from the sky. Zoë was curled up next to her as close as she could get, with Francis just as close on the other side. Snow had accumulated on them, making them look like a lumpy snowdrift in the all-white landscape.

Because it was already daylight, Millie half expected to find that Simon-Leo had gone to seek shelter from the sun, but he was there, feeding the fire and sitting exactly where he had been when she fell asleep.

"Why are you still here?" she asked as she wriggled out of her blanket.

"There's a snowstorm, if you haven't noticed," said Simon. "I can't see the sun, can you? We'll be fine as long as the snow keeps falling. Wake up, Leo," he shouted at his other head. "You like the snow. You're going to love this."

"Wha . . . ," said Leo, his eyes popping open. "Did you say there's snow?"

Simon smiled. Tilting his head back, he closed his eyes and stuck out his tongue. Leo copied him, smacking his lips as the melting snow trickled down his throat. "You know what I want to do?" he asked his other head. "Snow trolls!"

"Don't be such a baby!" said Simon. "We haven't made snow trolls in years. Next you'll want to have a snowball fight."

"Good idea!" Leo said as he reached out and grabbed a handful of snow. Simon's mouth formed an O of surprise when the snowball whacked him full in the face. He sputtered and coughed, then reached for some snow himself. Millie kept well away from the troll as the two heads pelted each other.

The sound of the troll shouting soon had Francis and Zoë up off the ground, although they kept their blankets wrapped around them.

Francis stomped his feet. "I'm freezing and we're not even in the mountains yet! It's only going to get colder," he said, glancing at Zoë and Millie.

"You could use your magic to get warm," said Zoë.

"So can Millie," he said.

"I can warm myself," said Millie, "but it's not going to do you any good. Why don't you make everyone some warm clothes? Zoë's lips are turning blue."

"I'm a knight, not a seamstress! I don't know anything about sewing."

"You don't need to," said Millie. "Your magic will do it all for you. Just try coming up with a spell that includes everything you want your magic to do."

"I guess I don't have any choice since no one else can do it," he grumbled to himself.

Simon shouted and Millie glanced at the troll. Leo was shoving his other head's face into the snow while trying to get rid of a mouthful of snow himself. Both troll faces were bright red and couldn't have looked happier.

"I have a spell ready," Francis said. "Now, don't talk while I do this."

A hat of fur, and gloves that will
Keep us from the winter chill.
Thick boots to make our toes stay warm
A cloak to block a winter storm.
Leggings make our legs stay cozy
Scarves to turn our faces rosy.
To keep us warm in this fierce breeze,
Bundle us in all of these.

Suddenly, they were all dressed in the warmest of clothes and no one was shivering. Francis turned a satisfied smile on his companions and said, "What would you have done if I hadn't come with you?"

"Mmph!" Leo muttered from behind the thick red scarf that now covered his nose and mouth.

Simon looked at his other head with disdain. "Did the hats have to have tassels? And what's that on my shoes?"

Millie glanced down at her own feet. The boots were made of some brown animal hide and were laced shut with a white cord that ended in fluffy white balls. Glancing at her friends, she saw that they were dressed in the same clothes in different colors.

"I like them!" said Zoë.

Millie thought Francis might have blushed, but she couldn't be sure because most of his face was hidden behind a bright green scarf.

"Well, I feel ridiculous!" said Simon. "I don't need these clothes and I'm not going to wear them!" He started to undo the fastenings on the cloak, but Leo slapped his hand away.

Pulling the scarf down from his mouth, Leo glared at his other head and said, "I don't care if you like them or not. We're keeping the cloak and the boots. These are the nicest clothes we've ever had and the first ones that weren't handed down to us from cousin Wartlips-Stinkybreath."

"I didn't think you cared about clothes," said Simon.

Leo turned his head away. "There's a lot of things you don't know about me."

Simon shrugged. "So, we'll keep them on. Are you people ready to go yet?" he asked, turning to frown at the others. "This storm doesn't look like it's going to let up anytime soon."

The snow had been falling steadily the whole time they'd been talking. Even the depressions left by their bodies had filled in.

Francis turned to Millie. "Which way do we go now?"

Although she already knew the answer, Millie checked her dragon sense one more time. "Through that pass," she said, pointing to where two mountains met high above them.

"I'll go first," said Francis, pulling his tasseled hat down more firmly over his ears. "Who knows what we'll find in those mountains."

Thirteen

Millie and her mother both suspected that Millie's limited magic was somehow bound to her dragon side. Like a dragon, she could perform simple magic without using spells or potions. Although she was hopeless when it came to changing objects or living creatures, Millie could make herself warm enough to dry her clothes or to stay cozy on a blustery day; she didn't need the warm clothes Francis had created. She liked them, though, and appreciated his efforts so much that she wouldn't have dreamed of turning them down.

Millie had other abilities as well, things that she'd never told her mother or her aunt or anyone else in her family. Just like Zoë could smell other vampires, Millie could sense the presence of magic. So when their hike through the foothills seemed to be taking an unusually long time, and they seemed to be climbing the same hill over and over again, Millie closed her eyes and listened. Under the whisper of the falling snow and the breathing of her companions there was a soft murmuring sound that she couldn't identify except to say that there was definitely magic at work.

Focusing on the magic, she decided after a time that it was old and had been in place for many years. It wasn't strong, but it didn't need to be since all it was supposed to do was discourage people from going into the mountains. It would be easy to turn it aside for the short time they would need to pass it. While her friends complained about their aching legs and rumbling stomachs, Millie walked in silence, suppressing the magic of the hills while letting her own personal magic guide her footsteps.

It was midafternoon before she no longer sensed the magic. When she opened her eyes she was surprised to see that they had reached the middle of a large mountain. The snow was deeper here, the air colder. Although her body remained warm and comfortable, she could see that her friends' eyes were watering and their cheeks were red. Ice was forming on the outside of their scarves. Millie was thinking about offering her scarf to Zoë when Francis stopped suddenly and exclaimed, "Will you look at that!"

Millie stepped out of the footprints her companions had made and peered through the still falling snow. At first she thought the figures were men. They were tall but rounded in odd ways. She had to go closer to see them clearly. They weren't real men at all, but snowmen formed from large balls of snow. Each one was holding a sign. DANGER! said one sign. GO BACK! said another. COME NO

CLOSER! DO NOT ENTER! LEAVE NOW OR FOREVER BE A FROZEN BALL OF ICE! The signs were large and written in bright colors meant to stand out in a world of white.

"What do you suppose this is all about?" asked Francis.

"I guess somebody doesn't want us to go up the mountain," Zoë said.

"The signs aren't just for us," said Millie. "Somebody doesn't want *anyone* to go up the mountain. You can stay here or go back now, but I'm not going to let a few signs stop me."

"Me neither," said Zoë.

"Of course not," said Francis.

"I think I should scout ahead," said Zoë. "You can keep walking and I'll meet you up there."

"Do you really think that's a good . . . ," Millie began, but Zoë had already turned into a bat and fluttered up the mountain.

"May I make a suggestion?" said Leo. "Simon and I should go first. Our feet are bigger and we can make bigger footprints for you to walk in."

"I think that's a very nice offer, Leo," said Millie.

With snow more than knee-deep, having Simon-Leo in the lead to break a trail for them made all the difference. They climbed the mountain more quickly now, despite their growing fatigue. Millie's dragon sense told her where the ice castle was located. What she didn't know was whether or not the Blue Witch was in it. While she and her friends slogged through the ever-deepening snow, she listened for magic again. It was there, right where she could feel the castle was located, but it seemed to be centered on a thing rather than a person. *How odd,* she thought.

Simon-Leo was plowing through a snowdrift when Zoë returned. The little bat came fluttering weakly toward them, her wings so stiff from the cold that they could no longer bend. "Help!" she cried, and tried to land at their feet but ended up in the snowdrift instead.

Francis plunged his hand into the snow, scooping it out until he reached the little bat. "Zoë, say something!" he said, sounding desperate, but all she could do was moan.

"Give her to me!" Millie said as Francis tried to warm Zoë with his breath. "I can get her warm faster than you can."

"Here," he said, handing the bat to Millie. A thin layer of ice had formed on Zoë's body and wings. A thicker layer glistened on her ears and chin. Zoë's mouth was moving, but no sounds were coming out as Millie took her friend from Francis.

Cradling the little bat in her hands, Millie thought about getting warmer. The temperature of her hands rose until they glowed. As the ice on Zoë melted, the water trickled between Millie's fingers, refreezing even before it reached the snow.

Francis hovered by Millie's side, peering down at Zoë. "How is she?" he asked.

"Give me a minute," said Millie. Zoë was shivering so hard that Millie's hands shook, but even that ceased as the bat grew warmer.

"I'm all right now!" Zoë finally called, pushing aside Millie's thumb to look up at her friends.

"What did you see?" Millie asked as she set Zoë on the ground.

"More snow," Zoë said, once she had returned to her human form. Pulling her scarf higher around her neck, she looked up at the mountain and said, "That's the last time I become a bat until we get to where it's warmer. I didn't think I was going to make it back this time."

Francis threw his arms around her in a hug, saying, "Then don't even think about doing it again. And don't you dare ask her to!" he added, turning to Millie.

"But I . . . It was her . . . ," Millie said, astonished. "It really was her idea," she told Simon-Leo as Francis adjusted Zoë's hat.

"I know," said Simon.

They continued on with Simon-Leo in the lead and Francis walking behind Zoë so he could help her over the rougher patches. Millie came last, smiling to herself each time her cousin showed his concern for her friend. She had never realized how much they liked each other.

After a time they reached a part of the mountain where rock jutting higher than their heads sheltered them from wind and snow.

"Look at that," said Francis.

Millie turned to follow Francis's gaze and gasped. A trio of snowmen stood frozen in the shelter of the towering rock just ahead. Unlike the first snowmen they'd seen, these weren't made from balls of snow, and looked amazingly real, as if they'd been sculpted in midstep.

Simon sighed. "I'll see about this."

The troll had just started to lumber toward the snowmen when Millie cried out, "No! Don't go any farther! They aren't snowmen, they're real. Look at the face of the last man!"

Just like Millie and her friends, the men were lined up in a row following in the footsteps of the person in the lead. Although his companions were facing forward, the figure at the end of the line was looking back. The expression on his face showed fatigue and worry the way a real, ordinary man's might. While her companions discussed what they should do next, Millie closed her eyes and listened for magic. It was there, a rough hum that made her feel edgy.

"Stay close together," she said, interrupting whatever Francis had been saying. "It'll be easier if we go through this all at once, so we're going to have to walk side by side."

"What are you talking about?" asked Francis.

Millie nodded in the direction of the pass. "There's magic at work there. I can feel it. I can keep it from hurting us if we hurry, but we have to stay together and we have to be fast."

"I don't understand," said Francis. "What do you mean you can sense magic? I didn't know anyone could do that."

"Well, I can," Millie snapped. "And if you'll listen to me I might even be able to do something about it."

"I think we should do what she says," said Zoë.

Grateful that at least one of her friends trusted her enough to listen, Millie said, "We're going to walk past those men without stopping. I don't think we have to go far to get past the magic, but stay together until I tell you we're safe."

Millie shut out everything except the magic. It lay thick on the ground in front of them, waiting to make each step harder until they could no longer move at all. She pushed against it with her mind, picturing it as a big unwieldy mattress that she was trying to prop up on its end, leaving enough space for them to walk by. It took all her concentration to keep the magic away, because it sagged in places and leaned toward them in others. She walked on, trusting in her personal magic to keep her on the right path, and had to fight to block out everything else when her friends started shouting. It wasn't until she knew they were past the magic that she let down her guard and looked around.

A snow leopard was crouched on a rocky outcropping about head-high just a dozen yards away. Seeing its eyes fixed on them, its back hunched, and its tail twitching, Millie knew that it was getting ready to pounce.

Francis had his sword unsheathed and ready when the

big cat leaped, but Leo was there first, grabbing the leopard around its middle and squeezing. While the leopard shrieked and spat, clawing at the troll's leather-hard skin, Simon tried to stay out of the way, ducking when a paw came too close. "What should I do with it?" Leo asked, clutching the writhing cat to his chest.

"Let me run it through!" said Francis as he closed in with his sword.

"No," said Millie. "Toss it!" And she pointed back the way they had come.

Leo glanced at her, nodded, and tossed the leopard toward the snowmen. The cat landed in a great puff of white as snow exploded from under it. Shaking its head, the cat turned back toward the troll. With its victim in sight, the cat took one slinking step, its belly brushing the snow. Its next step was slower, and the third never quite happened; the animal's front paw extended but was never set down. Even from where she stood, Millie could hear the sound of crackling as ice formed and the leopard froze, turning completely white from nose to tail.

"Are you all right?" Millie asked Leo.

"Uh-huh," he replied.

Simon scowled at him and said, "Well, I'm not. I don't care what you want to do, but I don't like to fight. I'd appreciate it if next time you'd consult with me before snatching up some ravaging animal who wants to shred us into table scraps."

"Sorry," said Leo. "It couldn't have hurt us, not really."

"That isn't the point," Simon said.

They continued on, catching glimpses of the top of the pass as they climbed. The wind picked up, whirling the snow around them as they fought to put one foot in front of the other. Hunching into the wind meant that they could stagger a few feet, but it would take them hours to go the short distance to the top of the pass that way, provided they weren't blown off the side of the mountain first.

"Maybe we can find a cave?" Simon said, turning to Zoë.

"Don't look at me," she replied. "Unless I'm a bat, I can't find a cave any better than you can and I'd freeze solid and be blown to the next kingdom if I turned into a bat now. What about you, Francis? Do you have any spells that could help us?"

"I've been trying to think of one. I suppose I could build a shelter out of ice, but there isn't much else I can—"

A roar shook the ground as a massive white-furred body slammed into Francis, knocking him into a snowdrift. Zoë screamed as another figure emerged from the blinding snow to pick up Simon-Leo and toss him aside as if the troll weighed nothing at all.

Millie glimpsed the face of one of the creatures when it suddenly loomed in front of her, standing taller than the tallest knight in her father's army. Its small, red-rimmed eyes were nearly lost in the shaggy white fur that covered its face. When it opened its mouth to roar, its yellow fangs were almost as sharp as a dragon's. Her ears still ringing, Millie ducked and rolled out of the way, trying to evade the beast's grasp, but then it had her and in the next instant she was flying through the air only to hit the rock and ice with a horrible thud. She thought she might be dead until she realized that she wouldn't hurt so much if she were. Struggling to sit, she didn't see the beast before it picked her up and threw her again. A moment later she heard Zoë scream and Simon's bellow cut short.

Suddenly, Millie was mad. It wasn't a gradual thing that took time to build, but a real, uncontrollable fury that snapped her from human to dragon in a heartbeat. Her wings opened with a crack like thunder and when she roared the mountain shook so hard that sheets of packed snow slipped free, causing an avalanche.

Using her dragon sense, Millie looked for her friends. She found Zoë, curled up in a ball of snow, bouncing down the side of the mountain. Millie scooped her up with her talons and held her close to her body, raising the temperature so that her friend could get warm. She saw Francis sliding feetfirst as he struggled to get hold of something to stop his fall. Millie caught him just as he catapulted off the side of the mountain into empty air, snatching him in midfall and holding him the way she was holding Zoë. Simon-Leo was harder to find, having been caught in the avalanche and buried under the rushing snow. Millie's scaled body was glowing with heat as she cradled Zoë and Francis closer to her and dove into the snow to pluck the troll from its depths with one of her hind feet. He thrashed and squawked as she flew into the air again, screaming as she rose higher.

"Be quiet," she said, curling her neck around to look at him. When the heads continued to bellow she shook her foot and added, "Stop that right now or I'll drop you."

Each head closed its mouth with a snap. The next time she looked back, Simon had his eyes squeezed shut, but Leo was looking with awe at the mountainside below.

With her friends safe, Millie flew toward the pass, circling when she saw the place where they'd been ambushed. The wind and snow had died away, yet no matter how hard she looked she couldn't find any sign of the creatures that had attacked them. She would have continued to look, but Francis groaned, bringing Millie's thoughts back to her friends. It was time to take care of them now. She'd take care of the white-furred monsters later.

Fourteen

Millie wasn't sure what to do. She had rescued her friends from certain death, but she had no idea what shape Zoë and Francis were in. For all she knew, they could die. When she tried to land, the ice beneath her began to melt and she had to flounder out of the pooling water, afraid that her charges might drown if she stayed on the ice for long.

Simon-Leo seemed fine, but neither Zoë nor Francis had said anything, which really had her worried. She supposed she could take them to the flatlands, but they were so far away. Even the foothills were too far.

It was nearly dusk when Millie saw the other dragon. She had flown over the pass in search of the ice castle, where she hoped to ask the Blue Witch for help, but before she could reach it, Francis had groaned again and Millie knew she had to set them down right away. She was looking for a flat rock big enough to land on when something flew so close that the wind of its passing knocked her off her stride.

Startled, Millie looked up from her study of the mountainside and saw a dragon unlike any she'd seen before. His scales were white tinged with blue, his wings were well shaped, and his body was long and sleek. When he turned and flew back to join her, she saw that his deep blue eyes looked kind and had the spark of intelligence common to the larger dragons.

"Are you lost?" he asked as he matched his speed to hers. He was about the same size as Millie, and his voice had yet to deepen into that of an adult male.

"I guess you could say that," she replied. "My friends are hurt. I need to land so I can help them."

"Follow me," he said. Tilting his wings, he turned and swooped across the face of the mountain to a ledge swept clear of ice and snow. "This is my home," he told Millie as he landed. "Or, at least, it is now." Glancing at her friends, he pointed at Simon-Leo. "I can understand being friends with humans, but that one's a troll, isn't it?"

"Unfortunately," Millie said as she dropped Simon-Leo on the ledge. The other dragon backed out of the way as Millie landed and very carefully laid Zoë and Francis beside the troll. She nudged Francis with her talon and was relieved when he turned his head.

"I think somebody hit me with a sack of bricks," he

said. Opening his eyes, he looked up and saw his cousin. "Oh, it was you."

"I didn't hit you with anything," Millie said, feeling indignant. "I caught you when you were falling to your death."

"Did you have to be so rough? I think you cracked one of my ribs."

Millie frowned at him. "You could say thank you," she said, and turned to Zoë.

"How is she?" Francis asked, and groaned as he tried to sit up.

"I don't know," said Millie, and nudged Zoë with a talon. When her friend didn't respond, Millie looked up at the other dragon with her brow ridges creased in worry. "I think she's unconscious."

"I have something you could try," said the white dragon, and headed to the back of the ledge.

Francis looked worried. He rolled over and got to his feet, even though it was obvious that he was stiff and sore. Kneeling by Zoë's side, he turned to Millie and said, "Will she be all right?"

"She will be if I can help it," said Millie.

Francis was watching over Zoë when Millie turned to see what the other dragon was doing. The ledge went farther back than she had thought, and opened into a cave. From what she could see, it was big enough to hold a dozen dragons and had another opening at the rear. Sacks and trunks were stacked against the cave walls and it was one of these trunks that the white dragon opened. He was returning to her when something in the cave moved and Millie realized that Simon-Leo was rooting through the sacks.

The white dragon must have seen the troll at the same time, because he glanced at him and said, "I wouldn't go to the back of the cave if I were you."

"Why not?' Simon asked. "Is that where you keep your treasure?"

The dragon snorted. "I wish I had a treasure. There's nothing there except poison gas."

"Poison gas?" Millie asked when he returned to the ledge.

"I sleep in that room. I've been so mad lately that I exhale poison gas in my sleep. Even a troll wouldn't last long if he breathed enough of it. Here, give your friend one drop of this. Two, if one isn't enough."

Francis hovered by her side as Millie took a small bottle of tonic from the white dragon's talons, pulled out the glass stopper, and let one drop fall between Zoë's parted lips. When nothing happened, she gave her friend another drop, then sat back to watch. Millie felt helpless with Zoë lying there with skin even paler than normal and her chest barely moving as she breathed. She wanted to do something . . . anything, but there was nothing, unless . . . Millie turned to the white dragon. "Can I give her some more?"

The dragon shook his head. "Another drop would kill her. Either this will work soon or—"

"Ooh, my head," moaned Zoë.

Francis sighed with relief. "Thank goodness," he said. "You had us worried."

"What happened?" asked Zoë. "The last thing I remember, those monsters were chasing us. One tossed you into the air, Millie. I thought I'd never see you again." Her voice was gaining strength as she spoke and the barest hint of color had come back into her cheeks. Suddenly, she looked like herself again.

"I saw it all," said Francis. "A monster rolled you around in the snow and tossed you down the side of the mountain, Zoë. I tried to stop him, but he knocked my sword out of my hand and threw me after you."

Zoë shivered. "I had the nicest dream, though. I was all warm and toasty. The air smelled good—not like here. What is that smell?" she asked, wrinkling her nose.

"I smell it, too," said Francis. "It's sour, with a real bite to it."

"I don't smell anything," Leo said.

Simon smirked. "You never do."

"That's the poison gas," said the white dragon. "It won't hurt you unless you breathe it in when it's concentrated. That's why I said you shouldn't go to the back of the cave."

When Zoë shivered again, Millie turned to the white

dragon. "Would it be all right if I started a fire? I'm Millie, by the way, and this is my friend Zoë, and my cousin Francis, and that," she said, pointing at the troll, "is Simon-Leo."

The dragon grinned and his whole face lit up. Millie's heart gave a funny lurch. *What's wrong with me?* she thought. *He's a dragon, not a human.*

"My name is Audun," he said. "You could start a fire, except I don't have any wood. I can get some if you want. I'll be back in a couple of hours. There are some trees on the south side of the last mountain in the range and I—"

"You don't have to go to all that trouble," said Millie.

"I don't mind," said the dragon.

"Why don't you just use coal?" said Leo. "I found some in a sack back there."

"What's coal?" asked Audun.

"I'll show you," said Leo.

Everyone waited while Simon-Leo trotted into the cave and returned lugging a bulging sack. "This is coal," Leo said, dumping the sack on the ground. "It burns like wood, only it doesn't smell so good, so I wouldn't do it inside the cave. We have a whole lot of it in our mountain."

"We'll do it out here," said Millie. "Maybe the fire will block the cold air from blowing into the cave."

Audun looked on while Leo piled the coal on the ledge. A puff of coal dust reached Audun, smudging his pure white scales. "My grandfather brought that with him. He was going to take it with us to our new home."

"What happened?" asked Millie. "Where is your grandfather now?"

"He's with my grandmother and my parents, locked away in a castle," said Audun.

"There," said Leo, "you can start the fire."

"I'll get two rocks," Audun said, glancing back into his cave. "We can smack them together and get a spark."

"There's no need," said Millie. "I can handle this part myself."

Taking a short breath, she exhaled a trickle of flame onto the coal, turning it a warm, glowing red. At the same moment, a line of fire raced from Millie's flame across the cave and into the room beyond. *Whoom!* Fire exploded in the back chamber, burning with great intensity for a moment and going out just as quickly.

"I guess your poison gas was flammable," she said, giving Audun an apologetic look. "I hope I didn't burn up something important."

"There wasn't much back there," he said, his eyes wide in disbelief. "How did you do that? I've never seen anything like it. That was amazing!"

Millie felt her face get hot. "All the dragons where I come from can do that."

"No one around here can. All we can do is breathe poison gas."

"That sounds pretty impressive to me!" said Simon.

"I guess it makes sense," Millie said, watching the water

from melted ice trickle out of the cave. "If you breathed fire, you would melt half the mountain."

"What else have you got back there?" asked Simon.

"Just stuff my grandfather collected," said Audun. "We were on our way to a new home when we stopped to rest. We were planning to stay here only a day or so."

The troll was already edging back into the cave when Audun glanced in his direction. "Mind if we look around?" Leo asked.

"I don't care," said Audun. "I already told you, there isn't much there."

Millie was using her talons to rearrange the coals in the fire when Audun turned back to her. "You can touch fire?" he asked, sounding amazed.

Millie glanced up. "Can't you?"

Audun shook his head. "Frost dragons can get burned just like most creatures."

Francis and Zoë got up to follow Simon-Leo, leaving Millie alone with Audun. "How did your family get locked away in a castle?" she asked.

"The day after we arrived, an eagle told us that a witch had built a castle near here," he said, his eyes growing fierce. "My grandparents went to see her. When they didn't come back, my parents flew off to look for them. I wanted to go, too, but my father made me stay here in case my grandparents came back. He said it was so they wouldn't think we'd left without them, but I really think it was to protect me.

The next morning I went to the castle and saw their claw markings on the ice. The witch had blocked the door so I couldn't get in and my family couldn't get out. It's been three weeks and nobody's returned yet."

"Where is this castle?" asked Millie.

"On the far side of that mountain," Audun said, pointing at the next mountain over.

"She wouldn't happen to be the Blue Witch, would she?"

Audun nodded. "That's what the eagle called her. How do you know her name?"

"She's the reason we're here," said Millie. "I came to learn something from her and my friends came to help me."

"If you're smart you won't go anywhere near her," Audun said.

"I have to see her," Millie replied. "It's why we've come so far and gone through so much."

"Do you know a way in?" asked Francis. He had come up behind Millie, but his eyes were on the white dragon.

Millie glanced at her cousin. "Audun says that we shouldn't try to see the Blue Witch."

"If we listened every time someone told us not to do something, we'd have turned back long ago." Francis held up a sword so the white dragon could see it. "I wanted to ask if I could borrow this. I lost my sword today and I don't want to go into that castle without one. You have a lot of them back there."

"Sure," said Audun. "You can keep it if you want to. It doesn't have any jewels on it, so it isn't worth much to me."

"Thanks!" said Francis, running his fingers the length of the scabbard. "This is perfect!"

"*Do* you know a way in?" Millie asked the white dragon.

"Yes, but you won't be able to use it. After the witch captured my family, she filled in the entrance so nothing bigger than a human or a troll," he said, glancing at Simon-Leo, "can fit through the door."

"Then I guess we'll have to wait until Millie is in a good mood," said Francis.

Audun looked puzzled. "What does that have to do with going to see the witch?"

Millie sighed. "I'm not always a dragon. I turn into one only when I'm angry. Usually I'm a human girl and could fit through that door."

"Did an evil witch cast a curse on you?" asked Audun.

"Nothing that simple," Millie said. "My mother is a witch who likes being a dragon. She was a dragon too often when she was expecting me, and I'm the one who has to pay the price."

Audun looked confused. "Do you really think that being a dragon is so awful?"

"It's not awful at all!" she exclaimed. "I love being a dragon! The only time I feel free and at peace is when I'm a dragon. It's just that I wasn't born to be one, not like you."

"So, about that door," said Francis.

"I don't like this," said Audun, "but if you have to go see her, I'll show you the door on one condition. Once you get inside, you have to try to find my family. I need to know if they're alive and if there's some way I can get them out."

"That's it? Go into a castle made of ice, get an evil old witch to reveal her secrets to Millie, then free some dragons who will probably spout poison gas at us?" Francis was practically sputtering as he looked from Audun to Millie and back again. "You can't be serious. It's bad enough that we have to go in there at all!"

"I don't know what else to do!" Audun told Millie.

"Of course, we'll do it," said Millie.

"Millie!" said Francis.

"We're going in, anyway, aren't we?" she asked her cousin. "It won't be that hard to look around. Between your magic and Simon-Leo's strength, it shouldn't be any problem to free a few dragons."

Audun's gaze traveled up and down Francis. "You have magic?" he asked.

"Yes, I do. So you'd better watch your step!"

Millie ground her teeth and glared at her cousin. "Francis, you're being rude!"

"Somebody around here needs to set this dragon straight," he snapped. "And I know *you're* not going to do it."

"How do you turn into a human?" asked Audun. "I wish I could."

"I have to relax," Millie said, "which isn't easy when I have such an infuriating cousin around." She glared at Francis again, but he pretended not to see it.

"And then what?" asked Audun.

"Then it just . . . happens," Millie said. "When I'm relaxed enough I think about being a human again, and I am."

"Can you do it now?"

Millie closed her eyes and tried, but nothing changed. "I guess not. I must still be too wound up inside."

"Can you hurry up, Millie?" said Francis. "I want to get this whole thing over with and get home before my parents do."

"You didn't get your parents' permission, did you? How old are you, anyway?" Audun asked him.

"That's none of your business," said Francis.

"Stop it, both of you!" Millie roared. "I'm going to go lie down and try to relax, which isn't going to happen if you two are fighting."

"I take deep breaths when I want to relax," said Audun. "If that doesn't work, I think about a place that I really like—one that makes me happy. That's what my mother told me to do when I was just a hatchling."

Millie found a comfortable spot against the wall of the cave and curled up so that her nose was resting on her tail. Although she didn't think she could fall asleep, she was so exhausted that she was soon snoring gently. When she woke a short time later, she saw Audun only a few feet away, watching her.

"That was amazing," he said. "One moment you were the most beautiful dragoness I've ever seen and the next you were the most beautiful human. You must have really powerful magic to transform that easily."

Millie sat up and brushed the hair out of her eyes. "I don't know. I can't control it yet."

"But you will. Someday you'll be able to do all sorts of things. I've never met anyone like you before."

"I don't think there are too many people like me around," she said, and glanced past the dragon to the cave opening. "It's time for us to go."

"If you're ready."

"I am," she said, taking the talon he offered to help her up. "I guess it's now or never."

Fifteen

Millie and her friends stood at the lip of Audun's ledge, looking down. A small cloud floated past beneath them and when it was gone there was nothing to see for a very long way. The ground was so far below that only a dragon could have seen a human on its surface.

"How are we supposed to get down there?" Francis asked. "I don't think even Simon-Leo could jump from here and live."

"You don't have to jump," said Audun. "I'll carry you to the castle. Millie, would you like to ride on my back?"

Francis glanced at the dragon's back and shrugged. "I suppose if it's the only way. I'll go first, and give you a hand up, Millie—"

Audun snarled and lowered his massive head so he was face-to-face with Francis. "I offered Millie a ride, not you. I'll carry you the same way you came here—in dragon claws."

"I don't think that's fair," said Francis, turning a little pale.

"Dragons don't have to be fair. It's the only way I'll carry you, but if you don't like it you can stay up here—forever. My lady," Audun said, lowering his neck so that Millie might climb onto it.

"Isn't there any way—," Millie began.

"No," said Audun. "I will not have that boy on my back."

"I'm sorry, Francis," Millie said as she took hold of one of Audun's ridges. "There isn't room for all of us up here, anyway. And you'll be perfectly safe in Audun's claws. I carried you that way myself."

"Where should I go?" Zoë asked in a small voice.

Millie glanced back and saw real fear on her friend's face. "Audun, do you think perhaps . . ."

The white dragon sighed. "I suppose I can carry her, but I'm not letting that troll climb up, so don't ask!"

"I wouldn't want to sit up there, anyway," grumbled Leo. "I'd probably get blown off!"

"The wind . . . ," said Zoë.

"You'll be safe," Audun replied. "Just hold on to my ridges and I'll fly slowly."

The dragon held still while Zoë climbed up behind Millie. When he reached for the troll, Simon closed his eyes while Leo watched everything with great interest.

"Uh-uh," said Francis. "You're not picking me up like that. Hold your foot still and I'll climb on."

"I'll have to tighten my grip so you don't fall," warned Audun.

"I know," Francis said, positioning himself so he could reach his scabbard. He tensed up, waiting for the pressure, and relaxed when the dragon didn't squeeze him.

"Hold tight," said Audun.

As the dragon's muscles bunched under her, Millie felt Zoë lean against her back. The great wings began a slow and steady beat, and suddenly they were in the air, soaring out over the vast emptiness that had opened beneath them.

"Wow!" Zoë breathed into Millie's ear. "I've never flown this high before. This is incredible."

"It is," Millie said, gazing around her in awe. Although she had flown alongside this same mountain only hours before, she had been too worried about her friends to appreciate the scenery. She gasped as the sun caught the snow on the mountains in a sparkling sheen of purest white. The deeper snow showed hints of blue, the same shade as the streaks on the white dragon. Tightening her grip, Millie glanced down. They were up so high that the river that ran between the mountains was the slimmest of lines. Riding a dragon was almost as exhilarating as *being* a dragon, although she would never have dreamed of trading one for the other.

They were approaching the next mountain in the range when Audun said, "Watch out. We're going up," and then they were climbing. Millie leaned forward so that she was hugging the dragon's neck, with her body pressed against the side of his ridge. Zoë bent over as well, holding her face against Millie's back as they arrowed nearly straight up. Even after Audun leveled off, Millie stayed where she was and was glad she had when he began his descent and the wind whistled past them.

She saw the ice castle right away; it would have been impossible to miss. The light reflecting off its surface would have been blinding if the sun hadn't been setting. The castle had been constructed in the cleft formed by three mountains. Like the surface of the mountains around them, the walls of the castle were white and blue. With tall, slender turrets and pinnacles, and lacelike arches that reached to the mountains themselves, the castle could only have been built with magic.

Millie's muscles were beginning to tremble from the effort it took to hold on when Audun finally set down Francis and Simon-Leo before landing at the foot of the castle. Zoë groaned as she slid into Francis's arms; Millie soon followed, her fingers still bent and stiff.

"The door's inside that archway," said Audun. "It's the only door in the entire castle. There are no windows or other openings. I know, because I've spent weeks trying to find a way in."

"How are we supposed to do this?" asked Francis. "Do we bang on the door or sneak in? I think we should sneak in."

"I say we barge in screaming and swinging axes," said Leo.

"You would," said Simon. "I think we should knock."

"For once I agree with Francis," Audun said. "The only way you'll be able to enter that castle is to sneak in."

"How will we get inside?" asked Zoë.

"That's easy," said Francis. "The door is made of ice. I could open that in my sleep."

"Then I guess this is good-bye," Millie said, turning to Audun.

"Be careful," said the dragon. "I know we've only just met, but I don't want to lose you, too. If you're not back in a few hours, I'm coming in after you. I can use that coal to melt the door."

"You won't need to do that," said Millie. "We'll be back before you know it." Standing on tiptoe, she kissed the dragon on the cheek and turned to join her friends.

"I can't believe you just kissed a dragon," Francis told her as they started toward the door.

"My mother kissed a frog," said Millie, "and look where they are now."

"That's different," Francis grumbled.

"Francis, half of the time I *am* a dragon. Do you really hate *me* so much?"

"No, of course not," said Francis. "But that doesn't mean I have to like the dragon who has his eye on you."

"Do you think he really likes me?" Millie asked.

"I don't get it," said Francis. "You'd have to be deaf, blind, and stupid not to see it, and I know you're not any of those. He looked like you'd cracked a lance over his head when you kissed him, he was that stunned."

Millie stopped and looked for the dragon, but he had already moved out of sight. When she turned back to Francis, he had reached the door and she had to run to catch up.

The door was only about five feet high, but from the depression around the frame it was obvious that there had once been a much bigger opening that had been filled in with more ice. With his friends huddled around him, Francis placed his hands on the door and muttered,

> Door of ice so white and clean,
> Open up for me.
> Let us pass within your halls.
> listen to my plea.

The door shivered and opened, letting a cool draft wash over them.

"That was it?" asked Simon. "That was the spell? I always thought spells were supposed to be long and complicated with all sorts of mumbo jumbo tossed in to make them sound important."

"I could do that," Francis said, "but that kind of spell takes a whole lot longer to make up. It's easier to make a mistake when you say them, too. I've found that if I keep my spells short and to the point, I get better, faster results. Did you see how fast that door opened?"

"If you don't mind, could you talk about this later?" said Millie. "The door is open and we can go in. That's all we need to know."

"Some people can be so grumpy," Francis said as he waited for his friends to go past. When they were all inside, he pulled the door closed behind him.

"Don't lock it," Millie whispered. "We might have to leave in a hurry."

The walls of the corridor were blue, as were the ceiling and the floor. Candles burned in sconces with a flame as cold as the walls. The corridor was bright from the light reflecting off the ice, but the walls were oddly shaped, with bumps here, dips there, deeper patches of blue in some places, and fanciful swirls in others.

At first Simon-Leo took the lead simply because he blocked the hallway with his broad shoulders and big stomach and wouldn't let anyone get past him. With his ax in his hand, he opened every door and peered inside, then shut it before anyone else could look. Francis was getting increasingly frustrated with this and kept trying to get past the troll, but he wasn't able to until they turned a corner and entered a wider corridor with even more misshapen walls. With so many bumps and bulges, it was nearly impossible to see more than a dozen feet in front of them.

Millie was beginning to wonder if they'd ever see a

living creature, when something stepped out from behind a bulge in the wall and almost ran into Francis. Millie gasped and Francis pulled his sword from its scabbard. It was one of the furry white monsters that had tried to kill them.

"Get back," Francis said, shoving Millie and Zoë behind him. "I'll take care of this."

"You and me both," said Leo, while Simon squeezed his eyes shut.

The beast opened its mouth as if to roar, then seemed to think better of it and closed its jaws with a snap. It watched warily as Francis and Leo approached it from opposite sides. After eyeing them both, it turned to Francis and knocked his sword away with one swift blow. The creature looked like he was about to tackle Francis when a cheery voice said, "Why, hello there!" Jerking its head as if it had been punched, the beast disappeared back around the bulge in the wall.

While Francis made as if to follow the beast, Millie turned in the direction of the voice. A little old woman dressed in a blue gown and a darker blue over-tunic was framed in an open doorway. She was smaller than Zoë and could easily have been mistaken for someone much younger if it hadn't been for the wrinkles etching the skin around her eyes. Her white hair had been done up in bows and curls that wobbled and bounced against her cheeks every time she spoke. Her clothes were clean and looked new, her shoes old and battered.

"I have guests!" she said, clapping her hands. "I haven't had guests in . . . Let me see now . . . five, no, seven . . . nineteen . . . No, no, that wasn't it. I know!" Her face lit up as she looked at each one in turn. "I've never had guests before. You four are the very first ones! Isn't this delightful?"

"Delightful," Zoë echoed as the old woman took her hand and started pulling her into the room behind her. It was a Great Hall, far bigger and more elegant than the bright and open Hall in Greater Greensward or the dark and dreary one in Upper Montevista. Zoë cast a pleading look at Millie and Simon-Leo, who were already following her to the door. They were about to enter the room when Francis returned, looking cross.

"What are you doing?" he asked from the doorway.

"You don't know how nice it is to hear another voice! My invisible servants are wonderful, but they never speak and I have been pining for someone to talk to. I talk to them, of course, but it's difficult to hold a conversation when you never know if the other party is in the room or not. Come in, come in! Supper should be ready soon."

The old woman pulled Zoë out of the way, then stepped back and waited for the others to enter. A creature much like the first snowman was about to follow them into the Great Hall when the old woman grabbed the door and slammed it in his face.

While the old woman chattered about how good it was

to see them, Millie looked around the Hall. There was one long table in the center of the room with dozens of chairs on either side. Nine of the creatures, or snowmen, as she was beginning to think of them, stood with their backs to the wall, watching the woman. One of them curled its lip in a silent snarl when it caught Millie looking at it, but it neither moved nor acknowledged her presence in any other way.

"I'm sure my servants will have plenty of food," said the old woman. "They always anticipate my needs and just now I need to take care of my guests."

Millie almost giggled when one of the creatures scowled and plodded from the room, taking great care to open and close the door silently.

A bell chimed softly somewhere in the castle and the little woman clapped her hands. "Dinner is ready!" she said, smiling brightly. "Now, my sweetlings, take your seats at the table. You can tell me all about yourselves while we eat. My name is Azuria. I'm the Blue Witch, of course. Oh, my, I have so many things to tell you. I've told my servants all my stories and I'm sure they're sick of hearing them, but now you're here and you haven't heard any of them. We could stay up all night talking and it would all be new to you! This is so exciting. Come along now! There we go. You take that seat, young man, and you sit there, sweetling. You'll sit beside me, young lady. And you, you're a troll, aren't you? You'll sit across from me so I can talk to both of your heads at once. Isn't this fun?"

At first Millie found the woman's ceaseless chatter annoying, but she soon realized that as long as the woman was talking she didn't need to say anything, which gave her plenty of time to look around. The chairs were wooden, as was the chest at the side of the room. There was a fireplace at the far end, but no logs inside or charring on the walls that would have shown that it had been used. The walls were blue and weren't completely straight, bulging in some places and bowing at others. A heavy wooden chandelier hung from an oddly shaped hook in the center of the room and the ceiling above it was blue in irregular splotches. The only source of light in the room was the candles in the chandelier and those set on the chest, but the light of the flames reflected off the walls of ice so many times that the room was as bright as daylight.

As Azuria rang a little bell the snowmen came and went, bringing in platters and refilling mugs. Their big, fur-covered hands were awkward, but they tried hard to do whatever the old woman seemed to want. Whenever the witch was talking to someone else or occupied with her food, Francis made faces at the snowmen, who made the most gruesome faces back. The game ended, however, when Azuria noticed a particularly awful face that Francis was making and asked him if he had a twitching disorder.

The food was wonderful, the flavors delicate or robust depending on the dish. It was so good, in fact, that Millie decided it must have been prepared with magic. Her mother had served food made with magic when they were on family trips. It was always delicious and served at exactly the right temperature, just like the Blue Witch's food. There wasn't anything wrong with a magical meal, in fact, Millie often preferred it, but it was interesting that the witch's food wasn't cooked in the normal way.

Millie looked up when Francis kicked her under the table. "Well, my dear," the old woman said, "is it a secret?"

"I'm sorry," said Millie. "Did you ask me something?"

"Your name," said the Blue Witch. "I've already told you mine, and your friends have told me theirs."

"I'm Millie," she replied.

The old woman smiled. "What a nice name! And what brings you here, Millie?"

"Actually, a friend of yours recommended that I come to see you. I don't know if you'd remember her, but her name is Mudine and she—"

"Mudine! Why, of course I remember her! She and I were best friends when we were children. We lived in town just blocks from the Magic Marketplace. My mother sold sweetmeats that enabled a person to speak any language she chose. Mudine's parents had a stand right across the way. They sold poultry. You know—geese that lay golden eggs, chickens that lay copper . . . When we were small,

Mudine and I spent our days playing beneath the stalls, watching for dropped coins and listening to the older witches talk about their magic. We learned a lot that way. Why, I remember, there was an old wizard who sold shoes . . . Here, would you like more soup?"

One of the servants hovering beside the table reached for Millie's bowl just as the old woman held up the ladle. Reaching across the table, she poured the hot, beet-red soup on the creature's hand so that it trickled off into Millie's bowl. The snowman didn't make a sound, but its mouth opened wide and Millie could have sworn she saw tears well up in its eyes.

"Everything is delicious," Zoë said from the other side of the table. She winked as Millie fished long white hairs out of her soup with her spoon and dropped them on the floor.

"If you grew up in the city, how did you end up here?" Millie asked Azuria.

"Oh, that's a long, sad story, but I'd be delighted to tell it to you," said the old witch. "I was madly in love, you see, but my beau was an unfaithful brute. When I learned what he had done, I packed my things and headed north, proclaiming that I was going as far from him as I could get. I ended up here in the midst of the most dreadful blizzard. I wandered for days and would have perished if my invisible servants hadn't found me and nursed me back to health. While I was regaining my strength, I told them about this marvelous castle I had visited when I was a girl. And wouldn't you know—they built this castle for me, which is just like the one I described. They've been adding onto it ever since. In fact, they built a whole new addition just a few weeks ago."

"It's beautiful," said Millie. "When Mudine said that you lived in the Icy North, I never imagined that your home would be as lovely as this. She said that you would be able to help me with a problem that's been troubling me my whole life. Every time I get angry I—"

"That sounds fascinating, my dear, and I'd love to hear all about it tomorrow. I know I mentioned staying up all night and talking," she said, stifling a yawn, "but I'm just too tired to do it tonight. It's time we all got some rest. But I must tell you that once I go to bed my servants blow out all the candles and the castle gets dismally dark. I wouldn't go anywhere after that if I were you. An ice castle can be very dangerous at night."

"But we weren't planning to stay long and—"

"Of course you're staying! As my very first guests, you can't just leave! You'll spend the night and tomorrow we'll have another opportunity to get to know each other. Now, if you'll excuse me . . ." Pushing back her chair abruptly, the old woman didn't seem to notice that she had shoved it into the stomach of one of her servants, who had been standing behind her. She tried to shove the chair back again and again, but the servant was doubled over in pain and the chair kept battering him, smashing his toes and pounding his shins. "Something's wrong with this chair," the old woman muttered. It wasn't until another servant helped the first one stagger out of the way that Azuria was able to put her chair where she wanted it to go.

The Blue Witch was already headed for the door when Millie and her friends realized that she was leaving. They stood, pushing back their chairs as the servants jumped out of the way. Millie was wondering what she should do, when Azuria turned back and said in a loud voice, "My guests need beds for the night. The girls should sleep in one room, the boys in another."

Her invisible servants stood poised to run as soon as she left, but Azuria no longer seemed to be in a hurry. "Sleep well, sweetlings," she told the four friends. "And remember what I said about staying in your rooms."

Millie nodded and said, "We will." She had no intention of wandering the halls in the dark with those abominable snowmen everywhere.

"Then good night," said the Blue Witch, blowing them each a kiss. "Sleep tight and don't let the ice bugs bite."

"Are there really such things as ice bugs?" Simon asked as Azuria left the room.

"I don't think so," said Francis. "But even if there were, they'd be the least of our worries."

Leo nodded. "Especially with those monsters lurking everywhere."

"I was thinking of the fact that I have to share a room with you," said Francis.

The room that Millie and Zoë shared was an odd shape, with a big bulge on one wall and a dip in the ceiling that brought the ice low enough to graze Millie's hair. It made Millie uncomfortable, although Zoë didn't seem to mind it. "My family spends a lot of time in caves, and they're usually pretty uneven," she said as she plumped up the heavy blanket she'd found folded on one of the two beds. "I've been meaning to ask, why do you suppose Azuria stopped you when you were trying to tell her why we came to see her?"

"I don't know, unless she really was tired. Maybe it's better this way. Audun thought she was evil and we don't know her well enough yet to say if she is or not. Are you sure you checked the room?"

"Yes, and so did you, at least a dozen times," said Zoë. "There's nothing here. Do you think I'd go to sleep in a room with those monsters in it?"

"I know. You're right. I just can't shake the feeling that we're being watched."

"That's not surprising, considering we have been ever since we met Azuria. I think it's a good thing she can't see them. Can you imagine what it would feel like to know they were watching every move you made all day, every day?"

"I'd hate it," said Millie. "And you're probably right.

Having them watching us for just a few hours has already gotten to me."

"I know we don't really know Azuria," said Zoë, "but she seems pretty nice if you ignore her craziness. Do you think she *really* can't see those monsters, or is that all pretense?"

Millie shrugged. "I guess she could have a form of snow blindness and can't see anything that's white. Otherwise the I-can't-see-them thing would be too hard to make believable."

Zoë stuck her head under the blanket and poked around inside it. "I suppose. And what about the evil part? I know the Green Witch is supposed to be the nicest, most powerful witch in Greater Greensward, but are all witches with color names supposed to be like that?"

"I think they're powerful, but I don't know about nice," said Millie.

Zoë's hair was a tangled mess when she came out from under the blanket. "Do you think she did something to Audun's family?"

"I have no idea. I haven't seen her do any magic yet, so I don't know what she's capable of doing. However, we'll find a way to explore the castle tomorrow. If there are dragons hidden here, we're going to find them. What are you doing? Are you going to sleep under that blanket or what?"

"I have to," said Zoë. "Just not like this."

Millie watched as Zoë climbed onto the bed and stood on the pillow. The air shimmered around her as she turned into a bat. The cool, dank puff almost made Millie sneeze.

"It's too cold in here to hang on to that ceiling," Zoë said as she shuffled off the pillow. "There are no bugs here, so I'm famished as a bat, but I can't stay a vampire with you sleeping this close to me. The temptation to bite you would keep me awake all night. It's bad enough that I can't sleep during the day without worrying that I might sleepwalk and bite you at night. Well, good night. To sort of quote Azuria, 'sleep tight and don't let the vampires bite.'"

"Very funny," said Millie, pulling her blanket up around her neck. While Zoë burrowed under the covers, Millie glanced around the room one last time. Although they'd both checked the room repeatedly, she wanted to make absolutely certain that there were no snowmen hiding anywhere, waiting for her to fall asleep. She hadn't seen any, but she still couldn't shake the feeling she'd had since the moment they entered the room that someone was watching her.

Sixteen

Millie woke the next morning to Zoë shaking her arm and saying, "Get up, sleepyhead. We have a lot to do today."

"You're up awfully early," Millie said, yawning. She glanced at her friend, then sat up to get a better look. "What's that on your cloak? It looks like white fur. That wasn't there yesterday."

Zoë looked down and began picking off the fur. "Let's just say I'm no longer hungry."

"You didn't!" said Millie. "And after we promised we wouldn't leave the room."

"I never promised any such thing. I woke up in the middle of the night because the castle shook and I heard this awful rumbling sound. I'm surprised you didn't hear it, too. By the time the noise stopped I was wide awake and starving. And since there aren't any bugs here . . . I'd never bite a friend or someone I really care about, but I don't like those fuzzy, white monsters. They aren't so bad, though, once you get to taste . . . I mean, know them." Zoë tilted her head and gave Millie an irritated look. "You should be grateful I did go out. Now there are fewer monsters to follow us around today."

"I'm surprised one of them didn't try to stop you," Millie said as she threw off the covers and reached for her cloak. "They seem to run in packs."

Zoë shrugged. "Actually, a few of them did try. I told you I was really hungry. I was mad, too. They attacked us when we were cold and unprepared. I thought it was time someone did the same to them."

"I doubt it will make a difference," said Millie. "But you never know. Want to go to breakfast with me? I'd like your company."

Zoë smiled, showing off her vampire fangs. "I'll go, even if it's just to see how many monsters are left."

There were four snowmen in the Great Hall when Millie and Zoë arrived. One of them, standing by the door, flared his nostrils and sniffed when Zoë walked past. She smiled at him and licked her lips. Instead of scowling at her like he might have done the day before, the snowman looked afraid and shifted uneasily from foot to foot until Zoë had walked away.

Millie was glad to see that Simon-Leo and Francis were already there, sitting at the long table in the center of the

Hall. She could see the steam rising off the porridge they were eating even before she sat down. "Did you sleep well?" she asked, noticing that Francis and Leo both had black eyes.

"No," Leo and Francis said at the same time.

"He snored," said Francis, pointing at Simon.

"I couldn't help it," Simon said. "I'm coming down with a head cold."

"We were talking last night," said Francis.

"Before or after your fight?" Millie asked.

"Both," said Francis. "We think you should ask Azuria the question you came to ask."

"Or get the magic doodad you came to get," added Simon.

"So we can go home," Leo said.

Zoë shuddered. "You're scaring me. You're starting to finish each other's sentences. Millie, I have to agree with them—I think we should go home as soon as possible before it gets any worse."

"Very funny," said Francis.

"I tried to ask her my question last night," Millie told them. "I'll try again as soon as I see her."

When one of the snowmen brought two more bowls, Millie noticed that he was careful to keep his distance from Zoë. He served them quickly, then scurried back to his place by the wall. Zoë handed her bowl to Simon-Leo, who was happy to eat her porridge. Millie noticed that the snowmen drew together after that to whisper behind their hands.

"I don't like the way the monsters are looking at Zoë," Francis said.

"She went out for a bite last night," said Millie.

"There you are!" sang Azuria as she breezed into the room. "Did you sleep well? I know I did. I like to sleep snuggled down under warm blankets in a cold room. Make sure to tell me if my servants don't take good care of you. I'm holding them responsible for your well-being, so let me know if everything isn't perfect."

"Everything is fine," Millie hurried to say when Simon opened his mouth. "We would like to look around your castle today, if you don't mind. And I really do need to ask you about my problem, so—"

"Millie, I'd love to continue our little chat about Mudine," Azuria interrupted. "Why don't you come with me? Your friends can explore the castle to their hearts' content. You can rejoin them later."

"I'll be right there," said Millie. Turning back to her friends, she said in as soft a voice as she could manage, "See if you can find the dragons. We have to take care of that before we can go home."

Zoë nodded and patted her hand. "Just be careful," she whispered back. "We don't know how far we can trust her."

The three snowmen who had followed Azuria into the room stayed with them as Millie and the old witch walked side by side down the corridor. When they reached the stairs, instead of going up as Millie had expected, the old woman led her down to the dungeon. "Follow me," she said, taking a candle from the wall before crossing to another door and another set of stairs.

They'd gone partway down when Millie glanced back. This time only two snowmen were following them, the third having stayed at the top. The stairwell was dark except for the light of Azuria's candle, but as they continued on, Millie was surprised to see that it was lighter ahead. It was warmer, too, and became increasingly hotter the lower they went, until the stairs ended and they stood in a cave glowing with a reddish light. Steam rose from the floor, and pools of water bubbled on either side of a narrow path. Someone had taken the time to encircle the pools with low stone walls just high enough to make comfortable seats.

Millie was still looking around when Azuria slipped off her shoes and lowered herself onto the edge of one of the pools. She sighed with relief as she dipped her feet into the water.

"Well, don't just stand there," said Azuria. "Sit down and take off your shoes. The water feels great, see!" Leaning back, the old woman kicked her feet in the water, splashing the path all the way to the bottom of the stairs.

Millie tried not to stare as the two snowmen scurried up the stairs and out of sight. "I dearly love a good, long soak," Azuria proclaimed in a loud voice as she continued to splash. Millie was wondering if the old woman had gone completely crazy when she finally pulled her feet out of the water and whispered, "Are they gone yet?"

"They just left," Millie said, and gasped when she realized what the woman had asked. "You mean you knew I could see them?"

"Of course, my dear. I've known for a long time that they aren't really invisible. It's just that my eyesight was damaged when I was lost in that blizzard. I couldn't see anything at first, but it's come back bit by bit and I can make out bright colors now."

"Is that why all the walls are blue—so you can see them?"

Azuria laughed. "I told my servants that I wanted them blue because I'm the Blue Witch, but that wasn't the real reason. I may not be able to see something that's white, but I can see the shape of it when it stands in front of a wall and blocks my lovely blue. They give themselves away in other ways, too. I can see their red-rimmed eyes and their fur when it gets dirty or stained. I can hear them when they walk, although they try very hard to be quiet. And I can smell them. I have a very good sniffer," she said, patting her nose with one finger. "If you ask me, they smell like wet dogs, which I never could abide. Now, tell me, my dear, why did you come to see me? You're having a problem with your magic, aren't you?"

"How did you know I have magic?" asked Millie. She sat down on the ledge and turned to face the old woman.

"Because Mudine would never send you to see me for anything less. I've been collecting every bit of information I can find about magic since I was a little girl. If I can't help you with a magical problem, no one can. So, what's wrong? I didn't want you to tell me while they were around," Azuria said, indicating the stairwell where the snowmen were waiting. "But you can tell me now."

"I need to learn how to control my anger. Every time I get angry I turn into . . . something."

"Ah, I see. Can you give me some examples of when this has happened?"

"It's been like this all my life, but lately I've tried to control it and I just can't. I lost my temper when I'd made plans for my birthday party and we had to drop everything and go to my grandmother's instead. And I really lost my temper when I learned that my grandmother had tricked and manipulated my parents into having the party where she lives just so she could show off for someone she wanted to impress. And then I lost it again when someone insulted a person whom I really care about. And then—"

"It sounds to me as if anger isn't your real problem. You've gotten angry over things that would have made anyone angry. I think your real problem is your magic. You don't need to learn to control your anger as much as you need to learn to control how and when you turn into a dragon."

"How did you know I turn into a dragon?" asked Millie.

Azuria tapped the side of her nose with her finger again. "I told you I have a very good sniffer. I can smell the dragon in you even when you're human, which means that your dragon side is always present. It isn't a bad smell. I'd describe it as hot and spicy, which is much better than wet dog."

"So what can I do to control *when* I turn into a dragon?"

"Do you have difficulty turning into a dragon at other times?"

"I can't do it unless I'm angry."

"And how about turning back into a human? Do you have to be angry then, too?"

"No, actually, I have to be calm and happy."

"I see. Come closer, child, and let me look at you." Putting both hands on the sides of Millie's face, Azuria drew her so close that their noses were almost touching. After peering into the girl's eyes for a moment, the old woman sat back and nodded. "Just as I thought. In order to turn into a dragon, you have to tap into your dragon magic. You must reach into yourself, find the fire that lies dormant within you, and coax it into flame. So far you've let your anger do this for you, perhaps out of an unconscious fear that your fire might hurt your fragile human self. That's why you've had to be calm to return to your human form. Don't worry; finding your fire *won't* hurt you. It will only make you stronger, because once you are able to consciously tap into your fire, you'll have much greater control over all your magic."

"I think I understand what you're saying, although I'm not sure how to do it," Millie said.

Azuria patted Millie's knee. "You will learn, my dear. Just give yourself a chance."

"I will." Millie stood and took a step away from the water. "Tell me something. Why did you want to come down here? Did you know your servants wouldn't stay long?"

"My servants!" said Azuria. "Ha! My *jailers* is more like it. I just call them my servants because I think it's what they want me to believe. You have to understand, they were kind at first and really did save my life in that blizzard. I was delirious for days afterward. I'd lost my sight and the feeling in my hands and feet. They cured me as best they could. In fact, it surprised me how well they did. I think it surprised them, too. Then they started to do other things for me, like build me the castle and cook food better than any I'd eaten in years. It was magic, that much was obvious, and it didn't take long before I figured out it was *my* magic. I'd brought an object of power with me, you see, and they had found a way to tap into it without actually touching it. After a time I got enough of my eyesight back that I could get around on my own, and I realized that they were watching me. Everywhere I'd go, they'd be there, watching what I did every minute of the day. Even the most attentive servants aren't that thorough, so I knew that something was up. They were after something, and it didn't take a genius to know it was my object of power. As long as they had me around, they could tap into the magic. But just think what they could do if they had the object themselves! They wouldn't need me, and they could go anywhere they wanted. So I tested them just to see what they would do." Azuria rubbed her hands together and chuckled. "I made a fake crystal ball and gave it a real polish. I treated that thing like it was the biggest treasure anyone had ever had and never let it out of my sight. Why, I slept with the darned thing and took baths with it and even sang to it at night. I must have had twenty of my *servants* following me around, hoping to get their hands on it."

"What happened?" asked Millie.

"One day when I knew they were all watching, I smashed it on the floor. You would have thought I'd killed their mothers! Some of them forgot themselves enough to howl! I had to come down here to be by myself so I could laugh till my sides hurt. They don't like the heat, you see, and they especially don't like hot water."

"When you splashed the water earlier and poured hot soup on that one's hand yesterday . . ."

"I splashed the water in case one of them was brave

enough to follow us down here. They stay near the top of the stairs when I get in a splashing mood. I wanted some privacy so we could have this conversation. And as for the soup . . . Oh, I do all sorts of things to those poor creatures just to see if they'll let down their guard and make a noise. I figure they deserve it. They've been driving me crazy with their snooping and their silence for years."

"Then why do you stay? Couldn't you leave and go live somewhere else?"

"And just where would I go? As old as I am and with half my eyesight gone, I'd have a hard time fending for myself anywhere else."

"I don't mean to be rude, but I don't think that's true. Mudine told me about a wonderful witch doctor who cured her of some terrible sickness. She's looking for someone to live with her. I know she's really lonely and would love to see you again."

"Mudine? You mean she didn't marry that old scalawag Olebald Wizard?"

Millie shook her head. "As far as I know, Mudine never got married at all."

"You don't say? Well, then, I might follow your suggestion and go see my old friend. Yes, indeed, that sounds like just what I should do." The old witch pulled her feet out of the water and turned so she could set them on the ground. Using Millie's arm to steady herself, she stood, saying, "So, now that you've got your problem solved and

I might have mine solved as well, maybe it's time we go back to civilization."

"That sounds good to me, except . . . What do you think your invisible servants will do when we try to leave the castle? If they haven't found your object of power, they aren't going to stand back and let you go. I know you said that they were kind to you, but they were horrible to us. They attacked us on the mountainside when we were on our way here. They tried to kill us!"

Azuria sighed and shook her head. "I was afraid they were doing something to make people stay away, but I didn't know it had gotten that bad. When I first came here I noticed a low-level magic working to discourage people from reaching the mountains. I thought they were shy and just wanted their privacy. But they must have taken stronger steps after they learned about my object of power, because no one has come this far for twenty years. It makes sense if you think about it. If they wanted to keep me until they found my object of power, they wouldn't want anyone coming to take me away or get the object before they could. If they tried to kill you . . . I shudder to think what they might have done if someone had actually reached the castle."

"But somebody did. Some dragons came to see you, and they haven't been seen since. You don't know if there are any dragons in your castle, do you?"

Azuria shook her head. "I haven't seen a dragon in years."

"Could your servants have used your object of power to lock dragons in your castle without you knowing it?"

"Anything is possible. The object is very powerful. Why? Were these dragons friends of yours?"

"They're members of a friend's family," said Millie. "Audun has been waiting for them to come home; he thought you were keeping them prisoner here."

"As far as I know, I'm the only prisoner in this castle, but you go right ahead and look for your dragons. When you've found them I'll have us out of here in two shakes of a dragon's tail. I know a lot more about how to use my object of power than my jailers ever did."

The snowmen were waiting at the top of the stairs just as the Blue Witch had predicted. They pressed themselves against the wall to let Millie and Azuria pass, but Millie didn't like the way they looked at her, and she began to wonder just how private her conversation with Azuria had been.

Shortly after she returned to the Great Hall, Millie's friends came in, talking about what they'd seen. For once there weren't any snowmen in the Hall, so she asked them how their day had gone. While Simon-Leo had explored the dungeon, Francis and Zoë had climbed the stairs to each of the towers and had come down shivering, saying that there was a snowstorm raging outside, but that they hadn't seen any dragons.

"I could find them in a minute if I had a farseeing ball like your mother's," Francis told Millie.

"Magic could help, if only . . ." Millie broke off as something occurred to her. It might work, but it would be easier if she were alone. "Please excuse me. There's something I want to try."

On the way to the room she shared with Zoë, Millie looked for snowmen, but they all seemed to have vanished. She wondered about that as she shut the door and inspected the room to make sure there weren't any lurking behind a hidden panel or hiding under a bed. What would make them change their habits so suddenly? Even if they had overheard her conversation with Azuria, why would they disappear like that?

Having made sure that she was alone, Millie sat on the bed and closed her eyes. Although she didn't have a farseeing ball and probably wouldn't be able to use one if she did, she had another kind of magic that just might help. Listening for magic on her way into the mountains had been easy. She doubted that listening for dragon magic would be very different. All dragons had magic of some sort, even after they died. She hoped to find Audun's family alive and healthy, but if she didn't, at least she'd be able to tell him what had happened to them.

Clearing her mind, Millie shut out the sounds of the ice creaking under the onslaught of the storm, the scrape of a bench in another room, and the beating of her own heart—and listened. At first there was nothing to hear aside from the background hum of magic left over from when the castle was built, but as she concentrated she began to hear another sound, a thrum *thrum*, thrum *thrum* that was amazingly strong once she knew what to listen for. Millie opened her eyes. The source had to be close by. In fact . . .

Fetching a candle from the hallway outside her room, Millie climbed onto her bed and held it up to the wall. There was something back there, something pale against the blue. Moving the candle flame closer to the wall, she followed the shape of the thing, trying to decipher just what it might be until she saw something nearly round and about as big as her fist, blue against the white—and it blinked.

Millie had found the dragons.

Seventeen

Millie found it hard to control her excitement as she went in search of Azuria. She had wanted to shout the news as soon as she saw the dragon, but she didn't want the snowmen to hear, although now they seemed to have gone somewhere and not come back. Although Millie knew she wasn't very good at finding people with her magic, she tried to focus on the Blue Witch. When that didn't work, she thought about the magic Azuria must have around her. This time, she found the old woman in less than a minute. Leery of alerting the snowmen, Millie didn't knock, but just opened the door and slipped through, shutting it behind her. The old woman was there, brushing her hair in front of a mirror.

"Good!" said Azuria. "You can help me with my hair. My servants usually do this, but they seem to have deserted me. I can feel my hair, I just can't see it. How does it look?"

"Here, let me," said Millie, taking the brush from the old woman's hand.

"Now, tell me why you came looking for me," said Azuria. "I can see by the expression on your face that you have news."

"I found the dragons!" said Millie. "They're frozen in the walls of this castle! That's probably why the walls are so oddly shaped."

"I've wondered why the servants add on to the castle when I'm the only one who lives here. They did it again last night. Did you feel the castle shake?" Azuria squinted at Millie. "Why are you standing there with a brush in your hand? Let's go free the poor creatures! This isn't going to be easy, so I need to take . . ." The old woman crossed to a chest and knelt down beside it. She muttered to herself as she rooted around, and finally sat back on her heels, saying, "This should do the trick." The vial that she held had a gold filigreed stopper that seemed to glow with a light of its own. After draping its golden cord around her neck, she shoved her hand at Millie. "Here, help me stand up. All this ice makes my joints stiff. Now, where exactly are the dragons?"

Millie braced herself and hauled the witch to her feet. "I saw one in the wall of the room where I slept."

"Then that's where we'll start," the old woman said as she opened the door.

They stepped into the hall so intent on their errand that Millie didn't notice the snowmen at first. When she realized that they were appearing one by one out of thin air, she stopped and put her hand on Azuria's shoulder. "They're back," she said. "They must have done something to make themselves truly invisible."

"Really?" said the old woman, placing her hand on her chest so that her fingers covered the vial. "Then they've learned how to draw more power from my object than I'd realized!"

The snowman closest to the witch smirked and reached out his hand. Millie noticed that his fur was smudged with a deep, dull black. *Just like Audun's scales when the coal dust blew on him,* she thought, and gasped when it occurred to her what that might mean. *Audun must have brought coal to melt the door like he said he would. If he'd gotten in, surely I would have seen him by now. But I haven't, which might explain why the snowmen were adding on to the castle last night: Audun is trapped in a wall, too.*

Millie was hoping that she was wrong when the snowman took hold of the vial and yanked so hard that the cord snapped.

"Ow!" cried Azuria. "That hurt, you buffoon!" The old woman struck out, but it seemed that she still couldn't see the snowmen because her blow merely grazed the creature's ear. Raising her hand to point in his general direction, she said, "You won't get away with this," and had just started to chant when another snowman knocked her to the ground.

"No!" Millie shouted. She was bending down to help

Azuria when a blow landed on the back of her head and everything went dark.

The first thing Millie noticed was the cold. She'd never really felt cold before because her metabolism was somewhere between that of a dragon and that of a human. But she was shivering now, which was a new sensation and one she didn't particularly like. Her natural reaction was to wrap her arms around herself, but when she tried, she found that she couldn't move. She wasn't quite awake yet, so it just seemed odd to her, certainly nothing to worry about. However, when she tried again and still couldn't budge, it bothered her enough that she finally came fully awake.

Something isn't right, Millie thought, and tried to open her eyes. They were as cold as the rest of her and felt as if they were frozen shut. She worked on her eyelids for a while, squeezing her eyes tightly shut, then trying to open them wide. When she got one partly open, she wondered if she really had because all she could see was a sea of blue. It wasn't until she had both eyes open that she saw something that wasn't blue, off to her right. She focused both eyes in that direction and realized that she was looking at a face. It was a large face and belonged to a white dragon. And then it all came back to her—how she'd found the dragon in the wall and gone to tell the Blue Witch and then been hit on the back of her head.

Millie felt another new sensation then—fear. Of course, she'd felt some kinds of fear before—fear for her friends' safety, fear that she might never meet the person who was right for her, fear that her parents would be angry—but she'd never felt fear for her life. Now, trapped in a wall of ice, she feared she'd never get out and would die there without anyone ever knowing what had happened to her.

It occurred to her that she wouldn't have to stay trapped in the ice if only she could turn into a dragon. The other dragons couldn't free themselves because they breathed poison gas instead of flames. If she were a dragon, however, she could free them all and then she'd teach those snowmen a lesson so they'd never harm anyone again! She was getting worked up over the prospect, but she just couldn't seem to make the transition. The problem was, she wasn't angry as much as afraid and worried.

Millie took a deep breath and tried to calm herself. She thought about what Azuria had said about tapping into her dragon fire. It sounded simple enough, if only she knew how to do it. The most she could manage was to adjust her own temperature and . . . Perhaps the two things were related. Could she have been tapping into her fire every time she adjusted the warmth of her hands or body? Maybe this wouldn't be so hard after all.

Millie closed her eyes and turned her thoughts inward,

searching for the source of the heat. There it was, deep inside her, a fire reverberating with so much power that she couldn't understand why she hadn't heard it every time she'd listened for magic. As she reached toward the fire she found that she could draw enough warmth from it to stop her shivering, but she could go only so far before the heat became a palpable force that pounded with the rhythm of her own heart, pushing her away with each beat. Azuria had been wrong about one thing: this was no ember waiting to be coaxed into a flame—this was a fire waiting to engulf Millie.

Reluctant to go any closer, she tried to think of something else she could do. If only she could get angry enough to tap into the fire the way she usually did. But she wasn't angry and trying to make herself mad hadn't worked. What if nothing worked? What if she couldn't change? What if she was trapped in the ice forever? Her parents would be furious that she had gone and worried that she hadn't come back. She was sure they would come looking for her, but unless they talked to Mudine, which seemed extremely unlikely, they wouldn't know where to look. There was always her mother's farseeing ball, but what if the snowmen could block it? She was going to be stuck in this castle forever, she just knew it!

If only she had never left Upper Montevista and come on this hopeless quest. Except . . . it hadn't really been hopeless because she had found her answer. But now, even though Azuria had assured her that the fire wouldn't hurt, Millie was looking for a way to avoid it. It wasn't the Blue Witch's fault that the fire was so big or that Millie was too scared to follow her advice. She could breathe fire, she could swim in fire, so why was she afraid of the fire inside her?

The thought that her own timidity might be holding her back was more than Millie could bear. She took a deep breath and looked toward the fire, resolved to do whatever she had to. Having traveled so far seeking the witch's advice, it would be foolish to ignore the witch now.

Determined, Millie started toward the fire. This time she didn't let herself think about what she was doing, but instead forced her way past the battering waves of ever-growing heat. Then, suddenly, she was through. To her surprise, the fire *didn't* hurt. The heat pulsing around her was invigorating and made her feel invincible—powerful, unafraid, and ready to take on anything.

This time, when Millie opened her eyes, she was delighted to see that although she was still locked in the ice, she was a dragon. The ice around her splintered as she shifted her weight, but she was still trapped and the pressure of fitting into a space that was too small for her dragon body was making it hard to breathe. The deepest breath she could take as a dragon wasn't very deep, but it was enough to allow a tongue of flame to melt the ice in front of her mouth. She struggled to take another breath; this time the narrow flame shot long and true, melting the ice all the way to the outside edge of the wall. She had fresh air now, although little space in which to breathe, so she took her breaths carefully, melting more of the ice around her with each exhalation. Water trickled out the hole in the wall, turning into a small river as the hole widened.

Once Millie had melted enough ice that she could take a truly deep breath, she began to work in earnest. She melted the ice behind the dragon to her right and was relieved to hear the creature free itself and scramble out of the wall. Knowing that at least one was alive gave her hope that the rest were as well, so she blew flames until she grew dizzy and light-headed. She rested for a moment, peering through the blue around her, hoping to locate another dragon. Instead, she saw Azuria and Zoë, shivering together in the sea of blue. Moving with great care, she melted the ice around them, then used her talons to break the rest of the ice and free them. Neither one was conscious. Millie laid them on the floor and went back into the wall to look around for others.

She found an elderly dragon and freed him, then continued on until all of her friends and the rest of Audun's family were either lying on the floor as they came around, or up and helping the others. Tired but happy, Millie went from dragon to human making sure that they were all right. When she reached Azuria, the old witch looked up and smiled. "I thought it was you. Glad to see you got that whole dragon thing under control. Did you get everyone out?" she asked, nodding at the dragons.

"I think there might be one more, but he wasn't near the others. Do you know where the snowmen went?"

"Ran off with their tails between their legs, if they have tails, that is. I've blocked them so they can't tap into my magic again. Should have done it long before this, but they were using it to take such good care of me that I didn't really want to."

"How could you block them? I thought they took your object of power with them. That vial . . ."

"That vial wasn't my object of power! My left shoe is," she said, lifting her foot and twisting her ankle back and forth so Millie could admire it.

Closing her eyes for a moment, Millie listened for the object's magic. It was there, a steady background noise that was so constant and pervasive that it was hard to notice unless she was specifically looking for it.

"They never did guess it was a stinky old shoe," Azuria continued. "That vial had some mighty tasty syrup in it, though. That stuff is great if you ever get a sore throat. I figured I'd need it once I started my incantations to free all the dragons. I wish I still had it. Sitting on this cold floor has made my throat hurt something awful."

"It's time you got out of here," said Millie. "Take everyone out of the castle and get them to safety while I look for Audun. I don't know if he's here or not, but I have to make sure."

"I want to get some things from my room," said Azuria. "That troll boy can come with me. He looks like he's strong enough to be of some use. Simon-Leo, come give me a hand! And before you go," she said, turning back to Millie, "see how that girl's doing. She looks awfully pale to me."

While Simon-Leo helped the old woman to her feet and supported her as they walked down the hall, Millie sat beside Zoë. Her friend was shivering in her sodden cloak, so Millie hugged her until both Zoë and the cloak were dry. "Are you all right?" she asked as Zoë pulled away.

"I'm fine," the girl replied. "Although I've never been so cold in my life."

"Where's Francis?"

"I told him I was all right so he went to talk to Audun's grandfather. They're comparing notes about the dragons from the different parts of the world."

Millie nodded, but her mind was already on something else. "I owe you an apology. I never should have let you and Francis come with me. I've put you both in danger throughout this whole trip."

"Don't apologize for something that wasn't your fault," said Zoë. "You didn't make me come with you. It was my decision, just like it was Francis's. And I'm glad we came. After hearing about our parents' adventures for so many years, it was time we had one of our own!"

Millie grinned. "I'm happy you feel that way, because it isn't over yet. You and Francis need to go with Azuria. I think Audun came looking for us and may still be trapped in the walls."

"Don't worry about us," said Zoë. "Go look for Audun. Just be careful. We started this trip with you and we want to end it the same way."

Millie had already listened for Audun while she'd been freeing the others but hadn't sensed any other dragon magic close by. While her friends made their way out of the castle, Millie paced the hallways, her head cocked to the side as she listened with more than just her ears. When she finally sensed something, it was so faint that she almost passed it by. It was less of a sound than a tickling, like the tip of a feather traced along her cheek, but it was enough to make her curious.

She studied the wall separating her from the source of the sensation. It was thicker than the rest, with a blue so deep in places that it was almost black. Try as she might, she couldn't see the curve of a sleek tail or the angle of the ridge down a back. Millie searched for the sensation again, trying to pinpoint it in the depths of the blue ice. When she believed she had it, she melted the wall in front of her a few inches at a time. Taking a deeper breath, she let out a bigger flame, but still the ice melted ever so slowly. She kept at it, however, until she thought she saw the outline of something. . . . It was Audun, she was sure of it, but a dark cloud swirled around him, making his figure indistinct.

As hard as she had worked before, Millie worked even harder now. She took deep breaths, melting the ice until she had almost reached the cloud. Audun hung suspended in the shifting vapors with his eyes half-closed. Millie listened again; his magic was fainter than before, as if he were fading away. Unsure of what the vapor might be, Millie stopped melting the ice when only a few inches were left and began scraping at it with her talons. When she finally broke through, she cautiously sniffed the air. Just as she had feared, it was the same smell that she and her friends had noticed in Audun's cave. It was poison gas, and from the look of the cloud swirling around the white dragon, it was very concentrated.

Millie knew that she had two choices, neither of which appealed to her. She could either melt the rest of the ice around him, probably igniting the gas, or chip away at the ice with her talons while breathing it herself.

It didn't take Millie long to make her decision. Breathing in the poison gas might kill her and then she wouldn't be able to help anyone. However, if she were to melt the ice and the gas did ignite . . . She'd just have to be quick, that was all.

This time, when Millie filled her lungs with air, she started moving before she exhaled. The ice melted in a blast of heat and she launched herself through it just as the gas inside turned into a ball of fire. An instant before the flames engulfed Audun, Millie wrapped her limbs and tail around him. She adjusted her body temperature so that she could absorb the heat of the fire with her back while chilling the side closest to him. The fire was fierce and hot, but it didn't last long. By the time it died away, the entire wall had melted, leaving a gaping hole in the side of the castle.

Audun was stirring in her grasp when she laid him on the ground and vaulted into the air. Although she hadn't been sure that she could take the fire into herself, now that she had, she knew that she had to release it before it consumed her. Choosing a gap between two mountains, she plunged into its depths and let her heat dissipate, melting the ice around her and creating a clear mountain pool.

Carrying the heat of the fire had left Millie feeling tired and weak. She floated in the pool, scarcely able to keep her head above the surface, and was on the verge of losing consciousness when she felt herself lifted from the water and carried into the air. "Are you all right?" Audun asked, gazing down into her eyes.

"I am now," Millie said with a certainty that surprised her. "How are you?"

"I couldn't be better," he replied, despite the singed scales that darkened his cheek. "Thank you for everything. You rescued my family and then you rescued me. I was coming for you when those beasts froze me with some sort of magic and covered me with ice. I would have been there forever if you hadn't come along. I can't believe you soaked up the fire like that. You have to be the bravest dragon I've ever met. Look, here are my parents. I want you to meet them."

Millie turned her head to look as Audun landed beside the ruins of the Blue Witch's castle, where his family had gathered. Like Audun, his family's scales were white, tinged with blue. They all thanked her effusively, but only his grandmother seemed to notice the tender way Audun set her on the ground when Millie swore that she was strong enough to stand, and how he wrapped his tail around hers in a proprietary sort of way.

The old dragoness frowned, but before she could say anything, Audun's mother stepped forward. "While we were trapped in the walls we saw everything that went on in that castle. You were very brave, my dear, especially for a human."

"Thank you," Millie said, smiling at the dragons. The only one who didn't smile back was Audun's grandmother.

"There you are!" Azuria shouted as she hobbled across the snow. Simon-Leo was weighted down with a huge leather sack and a rolled-up rug so long that the end dragged on the ground as he followed her. Millie recalled having seen the rug on the floor of the Blue Witch's chamber, but she wondered how the old woman thought she could possibly take it with them.

"That was fantastic!" shouted Francis. "I didn't know dragons could carry fire the way you did."

"Neither did I," Millie said.

Zoë looked anxious as she drew close to peer at Millie. "How do you feel? You don't look like you usually do. Your scales are still green, but they're kind of pink around the edges."

"I'm fine, Zoë. I just—," Millie began.

"First this streak of fire shot out of the castle and then it hit the ice with a *whoosh*!" Francis said, more excited than Millie had seen him in a long time. "We didn't know it was you until Audun brought you back. That ball of flames was you, wasn't it?"

"Yes, it was. I was just—"

The snowdrifts behind the Blue Witch exploded and a horde of snowmen tumbled out, roaring so loudly that Millie's heart skipped a beat. Azuria began to fumble at the sack Simon-Leo was carrying. Seeing that the old woman wouldn't be ready before the snowmen reached her, Millie leaned toward Audun and said, "Why don't we take care of this?"

Audun nodded and the two dragons took to the air.

While most of the snowmen watched them with wary eyes, some of their companions made great sweeping gestures with their arms and looked confused when nothing happened.

"I think they just learned that their magic no longer

works," Millie told Audun. The dragons swooped lower, making the snowmen duck. When Audun breathed poison gas in their direction, the snowmen grabbed their noses and pinched them shut. Although they had been prepared for a frost dragon's poison gas, they looked startled when Millie lit the gas with her flame. Howling, the snowmen threw themselves into snowdrifts, then ran away with their charred fur still smoking. When they were certain that the snowmen were gone, Millie and Audun landed, standing so close that their tails touched.

"I don't know about you," said the Blue Witch, "but I'm ready to get out of here. Anyone want a ride? Simon-Leo, you can put the carpet down now."

Simon-Leo grunted and dropped the sack so he could unroll the carpet on the snow.

"That can't be a magic carpet," said Francis. "It's huge."

"You bet it's huge," agreed Azuria. "I've had this thing for over fifty years and I spent a fortune for it. It can hold all of you, even the troll, although I draw the line at dragons."

Millie laughed. "I think I can get home on my own," she said, and turned to Audun. "I have to go now. I'm glad I got to meet you. Thank you for helping us. You saved Zoë's life with your tonic and you helped us find the Blue Witch."

"You don't need to thank me," said Audun. "You saved my entire family. You're a very special dragon, Millie. Are you sure you have to go?"

Millie nodded. "My parents are going to be worried sick about me if I don't get back before they do. Take care of yourself, Audun." Millie could have sworn that he blushed when she kissed him on the cheek. Simon-Leo chortled, but Millie didn't care. She felt as if she'd known Audun for years.

Although the carpet sagged under Simon-Leo, Azuria didn't have any trouble getting it to rise. "Now you take over," she told Francis, who was sitting beside her, his hand almost holding Zoë's. "The way my eyesight is, I'll have us crashing into mountains before you know it."

Francis looked delighted and didn't even glance back at Millie as he guided the carpet down the valley. Millie sighed and spread her wings. She took off, rising into the air to circle over the castle, then came back to fly low over Audun. "Will I ever see you again?" she called.

"You couldn't keep me away if you tried," he shouted into the wind, and waved until she was out of sight.

Magic carpets are very fast, but even the best magic carpet is no match for a flying dragon. Millie could have been back at her grandparents' castle within a few hours, but she slowed her pace to match that of the carpet. However, every now and then she flew ahead, lost in her thoughts, and then had to fly back to look for her friends.

The last time this happened was right before she spotted the mountains of Upper Montevista. It was late in the day and she would have preferred to go on, but she turned around to tell the others that they were almost there. Not everyone was happy to hear the news.

"I hope my parents aren't back yet," said Francis.

"What will you do if they are?" Zoë asked.

"Tell them about how I used my magic, I guess," Francis replied after a moment's thought. "That should make them happy."

"What are you going to tell your grandparents?" Zoë asked Millie.

"I don't know," Millie replied. "My father's parents probably won't want to see me. My mother's parents will probably be mad that I left the way I did."

"Are you going to tell your parents what happened?" asked Francis.

"Eventually," said Millie. "I've never kept secrets from them before. I don't see any reason to start now."

"We'll, *I'm* going to look up my old friend Mudine," said Azuria as her carpet skimmed above the top of the tallest mountain in the range. "We have a lot of catching up to do and I want to know if she's really looking for someone to share a cottage. While I'm at it, I'm going to ask her about that witch doctor friend of hers. Maybe she'd like to show me where to find him."

"I'm going to stay at your grandparents' castle for a few weeks until my parents are back from their trip," said Simon-Leo. "You don't think they'll mind, do you, Millie?"

"Oh, they'll mind, all right," Millie said, laughing.

Francis turned around to glance back at Simon-Leo, a guilty expression on his face. "You've been so quiet, I forgot you were there," he told the troll. "I guess I should turn around and take you back to where we found you."

"You don't need to do that," said Millie. "I think Simon-Leo *should* stay with Queen Frazzela and King Bodamin. Maybe after they've had a troll living with them for a few weeks, they'll appreciate a granddaughter who's a dragon only part of the time."

Francis snorted. "That's a great idea, but who's going to suggest it?"

"I will," said Millie. "And this time I think I can talk to my grandmother without worrying that I might lose my temper."

"Because she already knows that you turn into a dragon?" Francis asked.

Millie shook her head. "Because I don't think I'll turn into one unless I want to. You can't imagine what a relief it is to know that I might finally have a choice."